CUTE AGGRESSION

EMILY LYNN

PART I

SHE HAD GOTTEN INTO THE habit of bringing a hammer to school. Just in case, like a sanitary pad.

It had made her shoulders ache at first, but her backpack soon felt empty without it. On days like this, its weight was even comforting.

She climbed the stairs to the fifth floor. Her hammer thudded lightly against her back with every step. It almost felt like a hand, disembodied, patting her back in encouragement. It was the end of the school day, and she was going upstairs to walk by his classroom. She did this at the end of every school day just to peer into his window, just to see if he was there.

Her lungs and legs burned by the time she reached the fifth floor. The climb was never easy. It took her breath away no matter how many times she did it. She paused at the top of the stairs to regain her breath. She didn't like making noises when she breathed.

It was cooler up here where the wind could blow more freely. It made her skin feel less sticky. It eased her lungs, too. Her breathing slowed into silence again. She wiped sweat from her brow and began to trudge along the outdoor walkway. It was empty. Most students were heading home by now. If she looked out over the banister, she might have seen them leaving the school in hordes, cramming themselves into *songthaew*s or walking on foot along the surrounding grass fields. But she wasn't looking out over the banister. Her eyes were trained on his classroom.

It looked like his door was getting bigger, but she was only drawing closer. She felt like she needed to pee suddenly. It was from an impatient kind of anticipation. It almost felt like frustration. Good feelings could sometimes feel bad, she knew. Soon the door was so big it was all she could see. The window on the door came into view like the biggest TV screen. She peered through it.

He was there.

He sat at his desk before the chalkboard, scribbling away at a sheet of paper. The late day sun burned orange into the room through the back wall of windows. Through the door window, he looked like a serene painting. He looked like a military man in his teacher's uniform. He looked like a youth, studying. He looked like a whole lot of things.

She felt her insides curl, a familiar feeling. But then there was an abrupt shift in the familiarity. She felt a violent jolt, like an electric shock or a kick to the chest. Her brain was jostling her nerves, screaming to her that something was off about the scene. Something was different. She couldn't figure it out at first. Whenever she looked at him she saw only him. But that was exactly it, she realized. It was only him in that classroom. He was alone in that classroom.

He was rarely ever alone. He was well-loved by the students. When he walked around campus, they walked with him. When he ended class, they swarmed his desk like flies. He taught twelve-year-olds, and they were usually unabashed. They didn't seem to care he was sometimes awkward, that he often didn't know what to say. They only saw he was young and handsome and kind and could be anything they wanted him to be. A brother. A crush. A friend. A teacher.

She felt another violent jolt in her chest. An aftershock. And then her body was moving for her.

Her movements were quick and convulsive. She rushed, nearly panicking. She moved faster than she could think. She ripped her shirt tail out of her skirt—she was sixteen years old but she could pass for a big twelve-year-old like this. She dropped her backpack to the floor and squatted next to it. She unzipped it, shoved her hands inside, fished around. She pushed past her sketchbook and removed her hammer.

2

She reached behind herself and tucked the hammer into the waistband of her skirt. It was cold against her back and heavy in her skirt. It sent a chill up her spine, sweaty as she was.

She stood back up. She gave herself a headrush.

She opened his door. She walked right in.

She wasn't thinking, she was only moving toward him. She didn't even realize she had left her backpack on the floor outside. Her stomach was swirling now, like she was about to be sick. She was breathing hard again, hard enough to hear, and though she hated the sound of herself, she couldn't hate anything when she was looking at him.

He was getting bigger. He was all she could see now.

She approached him with her hands pressed together before her face with respect. He looked up at her. He must have heard her approach. Perhaps he heard her open the door. Perhaps he heard her breathing, too. When he saw her and her *wai*, he smiled at her. Students approached him like this all the time, but somehow the kindness in his smile never wavered no matter how customary that smile must have been.

It made her stutter in her step.

She was never used to him looking at her, smiling at her. It made her skin prickle every time.

Her skirt beneath her shirt tail was sagging with the weight of the hammer, and she quit her *wai* before her skirt could fall down. He didn't seem to notice how her hands flew to her waistband. He only smiled that same close-lipped smile, lips pinched like the inside of his mouth was something to hide.

He just kept getting bigger.

She was at his desk now. She was taller than him when he was sitting down. He was looking up at her expectantly, waiting for her to speak. But for a moment she didn't speak. She couldn't. The words got clogged in her throat when she realized, in all her years of knowing him, she had never before seen him at this angle. He looked younger like this, his chin tilted up like a child. He looked rounder, more three-dimensional. And in looking at him like this, it struck her that she was closer to him than she'd ever been. She was close enough to touch him, to see the little divots in his skin, to feel his breath on her face if he spoke. She was close enough to see herself in his eyes.

She flinched.

Her skin prickled again and she took a step back. At the same time, he straightened up a bit as though to subtly back away from her, too.

She must have been too close. She must have smelled like fish.

She swallowed dryly. She forced words from her throat. Her voice came out cracked from disuse. She couldn't stop the cringe contorting her face as she spoke. It was hard to talk to him. She hadn't talked to him in years. It was always unnatural, the thought of her voice in his ears.

She asked him if she could check her grade.

The term was ending in a few days. Many students were asking to check their grades.

He said, "Of course," and had been nodding before she even finished speaking. If he minded her contorted face, he didn't show it. He might have thought she was worried about her grade. He retrieved his stack of attendance sheets from inside his desk. "What class are you from?" he said, and there was a note of apology in his voice for not remembering.

She gave him a class number, a random one, the first she could think of. Her nerves were swelling now. They were making her vibrate. She wondered if he could hear the vibration in her voice. She cringed again.

He shuffled through the sheets. He found the class, then paused again. He must have realized he didn't remember her name. He looked up at her again, apologetically at first, but it quickly changed to a look of determination. "Wait, don't tell me," he said and squeezed his eyes shut and beat upon his temple as though that would help him remember. When his eyes flew open again, he pointed at her almost accusingly. "Dear, right?" he said. "That's your nickname?"

That wasn't her nickname. She nodded her head anyway, and he beamed. He had close to a thousand students each term. It wasn't possible for him to learn everybody's name, but he still tried. He wrote down the nicknames of every student in the margins of his attendance sheets, she knew. He had always been kind.

He went back to his sheet now, searching for Dear with his finger. Her own fingers went behind her back to work the hammer loose.

She hadn't tucked it well. She had been too anxious to do anything well. It was sagging so low and barely clinging to her waistband. She struggled to get it out. She had to twist her back to reach it and unhook it, and during her struggle he must have sensed movement. He glanced up at her.

She froze. She thought herself caught. She thought he had seen too much. She thought his brow would crease in confusion and then in alarm at the sight of her digging in her skirt. But there was no such confusion or alarm. There wasn't enough time. His eyes were on her for less than a second before he looked back down at his sheet and resumed his search for Dear.

He had barely even looked at her. He might have thought there was nothing to see. He might have thought she was picking a wedgie.

She swallowed again. Her throat clicked.

She was quiet when she removed the hammer from her skirt and quick when she raised it above her head.

Her heart was beating too fast. It was hurting her. She thought her ribs would bruise. Her hands were slick with sweat. She gripped the hammer harder. She aimed for the top of his head.

He shouldn't have seen it coming.

But it seemed he sensed some movement again.

As she made to bring down the hammer, he glanced up at her.

He saw her hammer coming down on him.

He flinched hard. She flinched even harder. But there was not enough time for him to dodge it, nor was there time for her to stop it.

He was struck hard upon the forehead, right above the left eyebrow.

It was a strong hit despite her sudden hesitation. She felt it all through the hammer. The hard impact of bone, the soft splitting of flesh. It made her own bones vibrate all the way to her shoulders. It made her own flesh shiver. It felt like she was the one being struck.

She thought that would be the end of it, that a stark silence would follow the blow like it did on the TV. But the sound of her hammer meeting his forehead seemed to evoke all the noise in the world.

The classroom was suddenly so loud. Upon being struck, he emitted from his mouth a cross between a gasp and a grunt—from pain or surprise or both—and quickly he began moving away from her. His chair skidded loudly across the floor as he stumbled. It screeched like railway tracks, like factory machines. It made her eardrums rattle inside her ears. It made pain erupt inside her head. He was moving away from her so fast, and amid the noise she tried to chase him, to hit him again, but he was too tall now that he stood and things were too loud for her to see. She rose to the tips of her toes and lunged at him almost blindly. She swung the hammer at his head again, but he only grabbed it and pulled it from her hands before it could even come close to hitting him.

The sweat on her hands was like lubricant. He pulled the hammer from her so easily.

She backed away from him. He backed away from her, too. He was breathing hard. He was nearly panting like a dog. He had the hammer high above his own head. It almost looked like he meant to bring it down on her head now, but he was only holding it out of her reach.

She stood frozen before him. She could only look at him. She was nothing without her hammer.

Already, he was bleeding badly. The hammer had opened the skin of his forehead. Blood poured from the slit and cascaded across his brow bone, down to his cheek. He looked very startled, very confused, like he had just awakened out of a nightmare, like he wasn't sure if the pain he felt was real. He brought a hand to his forehead, and when he saw blood on his fingers he only shook it off, like he wasn't sure if that was real either.

He blinked blood from his flashing eyes. Confused one moment, angry the next. She had never seen him angry before.

"What is going on?" he said. He was out of breath still, yet he sounded sterner than he'd ever sounded before. He almost sounded mean.

She was silent and paler than the one losing blood.

"Girl, speak," he said. "What is this?"

He looked at her so hard. His eyes on her felt like hands. It was like he was searching her face, trying to understand her, trying to pry her open and see for himself what was going on inside her head.

She couldn't stand it. She covered her face with her hands.

A silence followed. And then he softened.

He must have thought she was about to cry.

"I'm not angry," he said. He no longer sounded mean. He sounded more like himself. "I'm just confused. Please help me understand."

Still, she couldn't speak. She couldn't uncover her face. His eyes were still on her. She could feel them.

"Are you upset with me?" he said.

Over the sound of his panting she heard something wet. Through the cracks between her fingers she could see his blood dripping onto the floor. A small puddle was already forming at his feet. How could

6

the head bleed so much? she thought. It bled more than it did on the TV. It bled more than anything.

"Did I do something wrong?" he said.

The more he talked to her, the heavier his eyes felt.

"Did I give you a bad grade?"

She wanted to disappear into her hands. She closed the gaps between her fingers.

"Did I give someone else a bad grade?

"Yes?

"Did someone make you do this?"

He was trying so hard to make sense of things. He was making up his own story, a story plucked straight out of the TV. But she didn't like the stories she was in.

She sighed very heavily into her hands. Her breath quivered as it came out.

He must have thought she was really crying now.

He softened even further.

"That's fine." He was still trying to catch his breath. "That's fine, don't worry, just—

"Just don't hurt me," he said, and he punctuated it with a bashful kind of laugh, as though he weren't bleeding from the head, as though he weren't just attacked.

Suddenly, she smelled him. His sweat, his skin, his blood. She had never smelt his blood before. It had a metallic odor. She thought it was strange something that came from a human could smell like metal.

The smell of him kept getting stronger. It was enveloping her, and she realized he was getting closer to her. She might have run had she realized sooner what he meant to do. Instead, she could only freeze.

He gave her a hug.

He bled on her.

His body was so warm, his blood even warmer. But his embrace was brief, stiff, obligatory. She, too, was stiff in his arms. It was an unnatural embrace, as unnatural as her voice in his ears, her reflection in his eyes. His arms around her only reminded her of her own body. She wanted to fling his arms from her. She wanted to bolt out of the room. But she had half a mind to understand she couldn't. She needed to disappear another way.

Her muscles tightened as though to turn her body into stone, into wood, into something hard and inanimate. She remained still and

7

silent in his arms. She let him come to his own conclusions.

How could she even begin to explain she had hit him because she loved him?

~

There are many ways to take things. One could grab a kitten by the scruff of its neck and pluck it right out of its litter. One could pierce a fish's mouth and reel it in. One could shoot a dart at a stray dog, take its unconscious body. One could shoot a dart at anything for that matter. Or, like she had seen on the TV so many times before, one could hit a person on the head, or perhaps cover their nose and mouth with a drug-soaked rag.

~

Usually she was in no rush to get away from that school. Usually her walks home were long and slow and filled with daydreams that made her feel less like a person.

Today, she ran.

If she got home early and if she was quiet enough, she could sneak to the bathroom and wring Teacher's blood out of her shirt before her mother even noticed she was home.

The blood was all over her back, high up on her shoulder blade where not even her backpack could keep it hidden. She could see it when she craned her neck, splashes of red darkening the lavender fabric of her school shirt. It looked like someone had poured the blood on her from a bucket. Her mother was sure to see it. And how was she to explain it away? She couldn't blame it on a bloody nose. She needed to make it disappear before her mother even knew it existed.

She ran hard along the *soi*. Her hammer in her backpack slammed against her back the whole way. The school was in a fairly rural area, surrounded on all sides by long grass fields and flooded paddy fields. It took a lot of running before the fields came to an end and turned into the compact buildings of the sparse shopping district. By then she felt a bruise forming on her back where her hammer was striking her. She thought of Teacher. Was this how it felt when it had struck him in the head? How much harder would it have to hit her before she bled too?

She could hear herself wheezing as she ran. She had never run so much. She had lost her breath already. The air felt too humid to breathe. The orange sun which had painted Teacher's classroom was now red, and it felt like fire beating down on her. She felt her skin

8

burning. She felt sweat oozing from her until she was covered in it. She thought she might have sweated Teacher's blood right off her shirt. She thought she might have been dripping with his blood, leaving trails behind her on the sidewalk.

She could smell herself now. She smelled like sweat and body odor and fish. Soon her smell mixed with the odor of street food. She ran past a handful of vendors closing their food stands before nightfall. There weren't many of them. There was no business in this place. Their smoke stung her eyes and she moved too fast to see them, but she felt them looking at her. They could probably see the blood on her back. They could probably hear her wheezing. They could probably smell her, too.

Her skin burned even more. She ran even harder until she reached the apartment building where she lived with her mother.

The apartment building was isolated, located in a largely abandoned extension of the shopping district. It was surrounded only by empty shops, long deserted by their owners. The apartment itself had once been a shop before it was resurrected as an apartment. Her mother had said the neighboring buildings would be resurrected just the same, but she had been saying that for years.

It was a three-story French colonial tenement, sandwiched between near identical tenements. It had bars over its windows, and its white walls were stained black from wind-blown dirt. One would have thought a fire had burnt it. It had just three tenants, one on each floor. She and her mother had the middle floor. On the top floor lived an old lady. A drunk man had the ground floor, the floor which used to be a shop. The lobby walls were covered in his piss stains. He even left trails on the sidewalk outside sometimes, mapping out his trip to the nearest 7-Eleven and back.

She followed these trails into the apartment building now. There was no relief from the heat and humidity inside the lobby. It somehow felt even more hot and sticky in here, like the walls had trapped the wet air and fermented it. She clutched the stairwell railing and climbed the steps with her arms more than her legs. The muscles of her legs were uneasy, shaking, and her breath felt like heartburn. She reached her apartment. She opened the door slowly and with a certain amount of pressure so it wouldn't creak. When the doors of the apartment creaked, the whole building trembled. She slipped inside, and then she could no longer smell herself because another odor hit her in the face.

CUTE AGGRESSION

It was getting worse every day.

It used to sneak up on her gradually. It used to curl around her feet first, then rise and encircle her body like smoke until suddenly she found herself in its smelly embrace. But recently it had changed its course. It attacked, it didn't creep.

She exhaled sharply, fought back a cough, covered her nose. She closed the door behind her, and the smell worsened. She didn't see her mother, but she heard her making noise in the kitchen. She hurried on her tiptoes to the bathroom. She made it without being seen. She locked herself inside the bathroom.

She tried to peel off her shirt, but the fabric was entirely drenched. It was stuck to her skin with her own sweat. She had to fight to get it off. She was red in the face when she finally removed it. She threw it in the sink with a huff of frustration. She didn't like making noises, but sometimes she couldn't stop herself.

There was so much blood on the shirt, even more than she had thought. It almost looked like a pattern of red flowers on the purple fabric. She wondered if it could even be wrung out. She reached for the handle of the faucet, but just as she was about to turn on the tap, she stopped, suddenly paralyzed.

Her sweat was making the blood run again.

It was warming it, wetting it. It was like he was bleeding all over again.

Carefully she brought her fingers to it. The blood came off on her fingers right away. It was the color of rust. It mixed with the color of her skin and made it look like her fingers were blushing. She turned around, craned her neck, and saw in the mirror his blood was making her back blush, too. She rubbed the blood between her fingers just to feel it. It was sticky. Then she brought her fingers to her nose. It smelled like his blood had smelled in the classroom, like metal.

She looked at the shirt in the sink again. She still did not turn on the faucet. She found she couldn't.

This substance on her fingers and back was once wet and alive, pulsing inside of Teacher, flowing inside him with every throb of his heart. This blood had even been *inside* his heart once. It had been so deep inside him, deeper than anyone else could touch, and she was touching it now. She was touching him, and he couldn't even feel her on him. She was close to him without even being near him. She was close to him without him even knowing.

She snatched the shirt out of the sink.

She folded it carefully to preserve the blood. She left the bathroom. She snuck to her bedroom and wedged the shirt under her mattress where she kept her private sketchbook. Then she came out of her bedroom with no shirt on. She forgot about the bad smell in the apartment. She forgot about her mother. She forgot about herself too. She was distracted by the stickiness on her fingers. Teacher on her fingers.

She was still rubbing his blood into her skin when she ran into her mother.

They both jumped at the sight of one another.

She quickly hid her bloody fingers behind her back, and her mother made a frightened, strangled noise in her throat, then sucked her teeth in annoyance at having been frightened.

"You're early," her mother said, sharply sighing the fear out. "I didn't hear you come in." She was half deaf and scarcely heard anything.

The fear might have been fading in her mother, but hers only intensified. She expected an interrogation. She expected her mother to barrel questions, to ask her when she had gotten home and why so early. Her heart began hammering and her mind began racing with potential answers to potential questions. She hated interrogations. She opened her mouth to give an explanation before the questioning even began. But then she stopped herself.

She closed her mouth. Her mother did not intend to interrogate. There was something of more concern on her mother's mind, and it showed on her face.

Her mother said, "Do you smell that?"

~

For once, she didn't want to go to school the next day. She figured there would be trouble. She couldn't just hit someone like that and not have trouble afterward. Teacher could have told someone. He could have reported the incident to the director. He could have ruined her and didn't even need a hammer to do it.

She didn't want there to be any trouble. She dreaded drama and the attention that followed. The last time there was trouble at school was years ago. She wanted to keep that time the last time. She had been careful after that. She had been sure that time was the last time. But now, she feared, it might not be. All because her hammer had not done what it was supposed to do.

She had come so close to acquiring Teacher. She would have

acquired him, but her hammer didn't render him unconscious. It only spilled blood. And while she had managed to collect that blood in the fabric of her shirt, that was only one part of him she had captured when she could have captured all of him.

The sting of disappointment was perhaps worse than the dread.

She should have hit him harder with her hammer. She should have taken him any way she could.

~

The morning was gray and the air was especially sticky with an incoming storm. The school intercom system spouted the school anthem. It was ear-piercing. Anything coming from that intercom sounded like churning metal. She always wanted to cover her ears against it. She never did. The students around her didn't seem to mind the noise. They didn't even wince. They were busy making their own noise as they arrived on campus. They roamed the uneven paths of the school or congregated at lunch benches and alcoves, already sweating through their lavender shirts, already excitable and screaming at barely eight in the morning.

She pretended to not mind the noise. She tried not to wince. Only then could she begin to vanish.

She maneuvered unseen between the flow of students. She became more invisible with each person she passed. By the time the last tinny note of the school anthem finished, she had long disappeared. She had promptly folded herself into her usual hiding place, backpack and all. When the bicycle man came out, she was already well-situated and well-hidden in the ventilation unit.

The bicycle man did his rounds as usual. He rode around campus, shouting through his megaphone, herding idle students to the morning ceremony at the gymnasium. His voice grated her ears on a regular day, but today she could hardly stand it. She was anxious and impatient and felt like she needed to pee.

With great difficulty she squatted in her vent and waited for silence. She heard the bicycle man's megaphone voice dissipate along with the shuffle of the students' footsteps. The sound lowered gradually like the volume on a TV. She heard the morning ceremony commence in the distance, muffled and garbled.

She unfolded herself.

The campus was vacant now, but she walked a narrow path between the white buildings just in case the bicycle man came back for another round, which he sometimes did. When she reached the teachers' office building, she crouched in the nearby grass fields. There was a dent in the dirt here from her crouching every morning. She fished around in her backpack for her battered pair of binoculars. It was a children's toy made of cheap plastic. Its lenses were scratched, but they still did the trick. Her mother had bought it for her when she was a sick three-year-old so she could peer out the window at the world instead of going into it. She often couldn't go into it, sick as she was. She had been so sick she almost died.

She held the binoculars to her face now and aimed it upward at the window of a certain office on the third floor. The storm above was swelling, but not yet breaking. It lingered in the air and made the lenses of her binoculars fog up. It made everything blurry. It was like trying to see far through near-sighted eyes. She made a noise of frustration and wiped the lenses on her blue skirt. She brought them to her face again, and already the fog began creeping back in, starting at the edges, working its way in like a bad smell. But before they could become completely blurry again, she saw him.

Teacher. Her teacher.

Her stomach twisted with affection. Mixed with her nerves, her dread, her disappointment, it felt like nausea.

He was hazy through the foggy lenses, but it made him look ethereal. It made him glow. His face was puffy, as it always was in the morning, but he wasn't disheveled, he wasn't down. He came into the office smiling that pinched smile of his. He came in clean-shaven with his hair nicely gelled and parted, his tan civil servant shirt ironed and buttoned up piously to the collarbone.

He was unchanged except for a scab on his brow.

She felt a falter in her anxiety. Hastily she wiped the lenses of her binoculars again, thinking she wasn't seeing right. The steamed lenses must have been obscuring the sight of him. But when she looked again, she saw the same thing. The wound on his forehead had closed already. There wasn't even any bruising. In fact, his skin looked smoother than usual. The place where the cut had been was just red now. Swollen with a little crusting. It was barely even there. It might not even leave a scar.

Perhaps he had willed it closed, wanting to forget it all. Perhaps *she* had willed it closed, not wanting any trouble, because today he was miraculously normal. He was smiling and laughing with the other teachers in the office now. The trouble she had dreaded was nowhere to be found. She searched for it, for any little sign of it. She had gotten good at finding things Teacher was hiding. But now, she could find nothing. It was like the hammer incident had never occurred. And even when the woman teacher he was talking to suddenly pointed at his forehead, Teacher only widened his smile and shook his head.

Oh, this? It's nothing.

He mimed some sort of accident in which he hurt himself in a funny way, and the woman teacher laughed so hard she had to cover her mouth. People loved to laugh at Teacher. Teacher laughed along with her, his closed, quiet laugh, same as his smile. She thought she could hear it herself, but it was only the memory of it reverberating deep in her ears.

She let the binoculars fall back down to her lap.

She no longer felt like she needed to pee.

She understood clearly then. Teacher, having too much heart, would not tell anyone about the hammer incident.

She should have known. He had always been kind.

~

The storm finally broke. She was in math class, learning it was much harder to draw a naked body than a clothed one.

She knew by now there were certain times when she couldn't be with Teacher. When it rained, for example, she couldn't be with him because then she would be wet, and people would look at her and ask her why she was wet. Likewise, she couldn't be with him when she had class. If she had too many absences in her classes, teachers would start to notice her name on their attendance sheets. She found it annoying her lack of a presence could make people notice her. She also couldn't be with Teacher when he wasn't on campus. She simply couldn't. It was harder to spy upon him outside the campus because it was less controlled. There were too many variables, too many people with eyes, and she wasn't yet familiar with the hiding places of the world. She knew all the hiding places on campus, though. She knew how the campus functioned. She knew how to disappear into it.

During these times when she couldn't go to Teacher, she found ways to bring him to her.

She sat hunched over her sketchbook at the back of the class where no one could look over her shoulder. The classroom was dark. The windows were steamed up with hot rain. The only light came from the overhead projector where the teacher was working out math problems. It provided just enough light for her to be able to draw.

She was never any good at art. Her mother had bought her this sketchbook a few years ago, thinking she would be good at drawing since she was bad at math. But all her drawings looked like a child had drawn them. She was always too hard-handed. Her lines were too thick. Her shading looked like smudges. And although she had filled nearly the whole sketchbook with these drawings, she wasn't improving. Each new drawing was just as crude as the last one.

She didn't care at first. These drawings were for her eyes only. There was no pressure to be good at anything when no one was looking. She drew to preserve rather than create anyway. To preserve the thoughts and images she created first in her head so she wouldn't forget them even after they left her head. But lately, drawing had been making her somewhat frustrated. She was coming to realize that even if they were for her eyes only, the drawings would never satisfy her completely because they never resembled Teacher closely enough.

Her hand was already getting sweaty. Her growing agitation was making the classroom hot even with the rickety ceiling fans blowing. She readjusted her grip on her pencil. She was finding it easier to draw the blankets on the bed than the body atop it. She figured it was partly because she had never seen a naked man before. She certainly had never seen a naked man in this position. Her imagination could only help her so much. No matter how many times she erased and redrew, it looked unnatural.

She sighed sharply through her nose. She erased again.

Thunder groaned like a hungry stomach. She couldn't even hear the math teacher over its roar, not that she would have been listening to him anyway. She couldn't stand math. It brought out bad things in her. The last few terms she had been placed in special math classes like this one. These classes were better for her, not because she learned more, but because the teachers never bothered the students. This teacher, a middle-aged man, ugly, spent the entire term droning on to himself more than to the students. It didn't matter if the students were paying any attention. Everyone was going to pass the class as long as they showed up, and the term was ending on Friday anyway.

She shook her head, a harsh, abrupt motion.

She tried to shake the thought of Friday right out of her head. She had to shake hard. Hard enough to make her hair fly off her forehead. Hard enough to hurt her own neck. Tomorrow was Friday.

She erased again.

She didn't know how to make the flesh look soft. Flesh wasn't soft the way blankets were soft. In person, Teacher's flesh looked soft, but at the same time it was stretched over taut muscle. He was as soft as he was firm. It was difficult to capture that subtlety on paper. More than difficult. It was impossible.

She figured her drawings would never truly resemble him. It was beyond her ability. It seemed she had no control over her own hands, over what she was making. And what she was making wasn't enough anymore.

She felt the intimate swell of frustration bubbling in her chest, fizzing like a shaken soda can about to explode. She suddenly realized she was pushing too hard on her pencil. She removed it from the paper before the lead could snap off.

She took a deep breath. She tried to calm herself. She remembered what happened the last time her frustration had burst in the middle of a math class. That had caused a lot of trouble.

She put the pencil down on the desk and held the sketchbook away at arm's length. Her drawings tended to look better from a distance.

She squinted at the sketch.

Teacher, naked, bent over.

~

The bathroom Teacher liked to go to had four walls and no ceiling. There were trees surrounding the walls, their thick, waxy leaves bunched around the top of the walls to ensure privacy. She had learned long ago these trees were easy to climb.

She climbed one now at the back of the bathroom where no one would see her. The rain had since let up, but the tree was still wet and dripping. The soles of her shoes slid against the bark. Her hands, too, couldn't get a good grip on the branches. She found herself struggling to get up the tree. She didn't know if it was the dampness of the tree slowing her down or if it was because her muscles were sore from yesterday's run. Or maybe, she feared, it was her age. Things were different now that she was older.

Despite the struggle, her timing was still accurate. When she reached the top of the tree and pushed the leaves from her view, Teacher was just entering through the door.

She frowned the way one frowns at a cute animal.

She rested her arms on the top of the wall, then rested her chin on her arms. She looked down at him, like she had done so many times, and she knew exactly what he would do. He wouldn't look at the mirror. He would walk right past it. He would go straight to the urinal, and he would urinate. He rarely ever defecated at school. She figured he was too shy. When he was finished urinating, he would shudder and shake himself off. He would wash his hands at the sink, and he wouldn't look up. He would look at his hands the whole time. And then he would leave out the door he came from.

It was the same every time, but she never got sick of watching it. It was like a scene from a favorite movie.

From the top of the tree, she watched him come into the bathroom. She saw the familiar shapes of the sweat stains on his teacher's uniform. She knew the patterns of his sweat by now. The walk from the office to the bathroom always made him sweat. Her eyes followed him on his way to the urinal. It was like she was leading him there with her eyes. But suddenly, he lagged behind her line of sight.

It was almost like a TV glitching and freezing just for a moment, but the moment was long enough for her to notice. She felt a surge of anxiety, and her eyes darted back to him. She found him standing at the mirror.

Her frown was no longer an affectionate one.

He never really looked at himself in the mirror. He only ever looked at his reflection sparingly, with flickering eyes. She understood in a way. To meet eyes with him was intimidating, though she couldn't help but think if she were him, she would never stop looking at the mirror. She would live in a house full of mirrors.

But now he was doing something he never did. He was standing in front of the mirror. He was looking right at himself. He wasn't looking into his own eyes though. His eyes were angled slightly upward. He was examining his forehead.

Her stomach turned. He was looking at the blurry red wound on his head. It was barely visible, but his eyes went straight to it. He examined it delicately, like how a woman examines her makeup. And though she liked him best when he was delicate, she felt a disturbance arise in her at the sight of it. When he looked at his forehead, she wondered if he was thinking of her.

His glance at the mirror was a brief one. It was perhaps only a few seconds before his eyes left himself and he resumed his normal path to the urinal. But the disturbance still clung to her. He had looked at his forehead, but it felt like he was looking at her.

She watched him go to the urinal. His back was facing her now. She couldn't see his front. With the way the urinals were situated she could never see his front. Instead of seeing, she would listen to the sound of his urination, as though the sound of it would help her imagine what his front looked like. She listened to it now, and the familiar sound was like rainwater slowly washing away the feelings of disturbance, replacing it with a certain comfort. But the comfort was only brief. Suddenly she felt like she needed to use the bathroom too. Sometimes it was like that. She was just that close to him, that connected. But this time was somehow different.

She realized it was only sadness cramping up her stomach.

Already he was shivering and shaking himself off. Soon he would be washing his hands, and soon after that he would be leaving out the bathroom door.

She wished she could make that door disappear. Will it away like she had willed away that wound her hammer had made. Then she could look at him like this forever.

~

There was great commotion at the fish factory today.

She had been working there with her mother for a year now. She only worked there on some days after school while her mother worked there full time. Her mother thought the part time work would be good for her. She didn't have friends. She didn't participate in extracurricular activities. She didn't appear interested in boys. She didn't appear interested in anything really. And while her mother respected this part of her, was perhaps grateful for this part of her, her mother also insisted she was now old enough to be more productive with her time. Money was the most concrete proof of productivity.

She didn't want to do it at first. When she said so, her mother told her life was a series of doing things she didn't want to do.

Typically it was mundane business at the factory. She and her mother worked at the gutting station on the second floor. They would stand at a conveyor belt and gut the fish that came to them. They would cut them apart and pluck out the bones. They would salvage all the soft parts and slop them into buckets so they could be sent to the mashing station and then to the canning station. It was tough at first. There were so many sharp things among the flesh. She had poked herself with fish bones many times. Sometimes she even bled. But once she had gotten familiar with the fish parts and the way they cleaved, she learned she could retreat into her head as her hands worked for her. With her eyes she saw bones and blood and little bodies reduced to meat. But with her mind's eye she saw Teacher in every way she wanted to see him.

She ended up not minding such work.

It was quite smelly though.

The fish smell was hard to wash off. She constantly smelled like fish now, but her mother always said there were worse things to smell like. Most people didn't notice the smell unless she got too close to them anyway. She made sure not to get too close.

The factory was an attack on all the senses, not just the sense of smell. The machines were so loud they left imprints on her. She could still hear them even when she was in total silence, like how bright lights leave stains on the vision. She figured that was why her mother was so hard of hearing. She figured she'd be the same after a couple years. That bothered her a bit, but she supposed she'd rather be deaf than blind.

Today, however, the immense noise of the factory was weaker than usual. It sounded like one of the many machines had been powered off. When she and her mother walked inside the factory, she saw a crowd gathered on the ground floor near the conveyor belts of the canning station. There were medics everywhere and a gurney nearby. Underneath the sound of the medics talking, she could just make out the sound of groaning. It almost sounded like a machine at first, like a cog churning, squealing. But she peeked over shoulders and saw it wasn't a machine making that noise. It was a factory woman caught in a machine.

What a mess it was. Long black hair was tangled in the gears, dragging half a scalp along with it. The forehead was pulled and ripped away just above the eyebrows, the skin peeling upward, making the factory woman look surprised. But despite the surprised expression, the factory woman was moaning like a machine and weeping in a way she'd never heard anyone weep. The woman's hand, too, was stuck in the gears. It was now bent unnaturally at the wrist. It was as though she had attempted to pull her hair out of the gears, but the machine had only consumed her hand along with her hair. The machine had evidently been stopped before it could consume any more of her.

The medics around the woman were conversing with one another, trying to figure out how to get her out in one piece. They were currently considering amputation, and the factory woman, still lucid, began wailing, to which a medic said, "Shit, I shouldn't have said that right in her ear."

All the while, she couldn't stop staring at the blood on the factory woman's scalped forehead. Blood upon her forehead not unlike Teacher's.

She found herself salivating at the sight of this mangled woman.

When she became aware of this pool in her mouth, she was embarrassed. She swallowed so hard she nearly choked, but already the pool was forming again. Quickly, she reached for her mother and tugged her along by the arm all the way to their gutting station. Her mother allowed herself to be tugged, perhaps thinking her daughter was disturbed by the sight of the accident. But in her head all she saw was the open wound she had created on Teacher's forehead, blood pouring down his face in that classroom, the smell of it like metal from a machine. The salivary glands in her throat felt about to burst.

~

Teacher. Her teacher. He could make even blood look sweet.

He was only her teacher once before, only for one term when she was just twelve years old, and that had been nothing short of a miracle. She was usually much too slow for classes like his. She was still not entirely convinced her placement in his class wasn't some sort of mistake. Or perhaps it was a case of divine intervention because nothing was the same after she saw Teacher for the first time.

She saw him for the first time and at once she was liberated.

It was first period on the first day of the term, the first day of secondary school. Primary school had ended badly, and already she couldn't help but believe secondary school's end would be even worse.

The classroom was alive with restless chatter, louder than primary school had ever been. It was packed full of forty twelve-year-olds, all either excited or terrified for their first day, all either glad or dismayed they were to have history first thing in the morning all term. She sat in the middle of them all. She had arrived too late to sit anywhere else. As their noises surrounded her and drilled into her ears, she looked at them, at each one of them, and slowly she felt herself stiffen. Her body had become corpselike, as though afflicted with a bout of premature rigor mortis, but her mind was alive and flooding with dreaded thoughts and images of all the friendships and acquaintances she would have to make.

She was not incapable of forming relationships. She could put on a face just as well as anyone else. It was always uncomfortable though. As she got older, she wondered where this discomfort came from and why it seemed to afflict only her. By the time she turned twelve, she came to a conclusion.

She was convinced all relationships were symbiotic. That to enter into a relationship was to subject oneself to a constant cycle of taking and being taken from. And from what she observed, many were content to be thrown into such a cycle. Not just content, but willing. They were seeking out such cycles, thirsting for them, throwing themselves into them. They wanted to be taken from, if only to get something in return. Perhaps the giving and taking balanced each other out.

The problem was she couldn't stand being taken from.

She preferred to be a passerby, completely removed from all perception, even her own.

That is not to say she was a girl without desires. She had plenty of desires. But all of them were beyond herself. They excluded herself. She only wished to see things. To see things but not be seen herself. To touch things but not be touched herself. To take things and not be taken from. And as she looked around the *mathayom* one classroom, all she saw were people who would see her and touch her and take from her. It was like they were already seeing her, touching her, taking from her. It was like she already knew them, and they already knew her.

She was tired, burdened just from a few minutes of being in class. She couldn't fathom six years of it. As the classroom's noise grew, her dread grew alongside it. It all amalgamated into one great, meaningless white noise. In her stiffened body she closed her eyes and tried to sink into it, disappear into it, drown in it, commit suicide into it.

Then, Teacher walked into the classroom.

His appearance put a dent in their noise.

The students in the front saw him and fell silent. When he greeted the class, more students fell silent. Some girls had even gasped themselves into silence. It was then when she opened her eyes again. It was then when she saw him for the first time.

Immediately, her eyes seemed to adhere to him. She couldn't look away. It was like she had no eyelids to blink. The only awareness of her own body came from the inside. The sight of him made her intestines feel like they were twisting inside her, a feeling she only ever felt before while looking at cute animals.

He was cuter than any animal.

He looked as young as a student. Had he worn a student uniform he would have fit right in with the older kids in *mathayom* six. But he wore a tan teacher's uniform and it fit him well, almost like a layer of skin. His skin was darker than the uniform. His skin was olive, like some green-brown trout. It made him look healthy, alive. It made him look like he spent time outside, not to work but to play. He looked like he played sports. He looked like he had muscle under his teacher's uniform. He looked like he had the body of a youth who could run and climb and throw but could still be overpowered by a man.

He was standing at the front of the classroom now. He was speaking about the class, about what to expect throughout the term, but she wasn't listening. She couldn't hear a thing. To look at him was to go deaf. To look at him was to have no ears, no body, only eyes.

Her eyes were fixed on his mouth. He opened his mouth very little as he spoke. His lips looked fleshy and soft, like a squishy toy made to be squeezed. But strangely his lips were pinched as they contorted into words she couldn't hear. It was a smile, she realized. He was smiling as he spoke, but it was a tight smile, a suppressed one. The corners of his lips were turning downward instead of upward. It would have looked more like a frown if it weren't for his eyes. It was like his eyes were smiling on their own.

And suddenly his smiling eyes were looking straight at hers.

She and Teacher only met eyes for a moment. It was a brief, unseeing glance on his part, the type of glances teachers do when addressing a large group of students. Had she been another girl, she might have blushed. She might have smiled. She might have felt special.

Instead, she felt queasy.

She flinched. She blinked hard. She remembered she had eyelids. She remembered she had a body, one that could also be looked at. She looked away. It felt like ice water was spidering through her veins. Her skin prickled into gooseflesh.

It was weird, him meeting eyes with her. It was almost scary. It was like a character in a movie had suddenly seen her watching him through the screen.

She sat for a moment paralyzed in her seat, looking down at her hands in her lap. She suddenly found she could hear again. The students around her were excited, loud again, but in a different way. They were battering Teacher with questions. They were fixated now on how young he was. He looked to be only twenty. When asked, he said he was twenty-three.

"Teacher, you're younger than my brother!" one student exclaimed. The classroom erupted with laughter, and Teacher laughed along with them. Somehow she didn't hear anything except Teacher's laugh, though it was quiet, almost silent. It was a cute laugh, deep as his voice and squeaky in his throat and strangely suppressed, just like his smile.

It made her want to look at him again. See that smile again.

She lifted her eyes carefully. He was no longer looking at her. Already, she couldn't look away, even with the threat of him meeting eyes with her again. Already, she felt the curling in her stomach again. Her insides were twisting so hard she thought she would hear them squelching inside her. It was almost painful, this affection she felt. It was almost aggressive. Her hands in her lap turned to fists, like she wanted to squeeze something. Her teeth clenched behind her lips. She wanted to bite something too. But then it began to evolve. It felt like a sickness now. Like a disease. So much blood pumped through her veins. Her heart beat so fast, her head was swimming. Her face felt hot, but from the inside, like her skull was on fire. It was like a fever suddenly wrought upon her. It was like she was a sick kid again, wrapped up in blankets at home and watching all the TV shows she would have missed had she been well.

There was something addictive about feeling sick. Something comforting about a fever.

Her eyes on him were like a tongue prodding at an aching tooth, and as she prodded him and relished in the strangely pleasurable pain, she found herself more confused by him than anything. Just by walking into that classroom he had evoked something in her no one else had before. There was no boy that made her feel the way Teacher made her feel. She supposed she didn't like Teacher the way a girl likes a boy. She didn't like him the way a girl likes her teacher either. She liked him the way a girl likes the posters on her wall, the singers in her favorite band, the actors on her TV. He was someone she could look at, but someone who wasn't meant to look back at her.

Her insides twisted just a little tighter. She realized she was looking at someone very special. She realized she would never need to make another friend ever again in her life.

When class was over, Teacher left the classroom but somehow stayed with her.

~

Her affection only grew, very much like a disease. Even as years passed, even when she was no longer his student, it only became even more painful, more aggressive. She wasn't just clenching her fists; she was digging her nails into her palms. She wasn't just grinding her teeth; she was biting the tip of her tongue. She longed for the fever-like symptoms his appearance caused in her. The flood of blood in her veins, the curling in her stomach one step away from nausea. It was addictive, and she sought it out any way she could. She stared at him in class when she was in his class. Then, when that term was over, she stared at him through her binoculars. She followed him around campus, to his classrooms, to the canteen, to the bathroom, to the teacher's office. She was no longer a part of the school the way she was meant to be. She was no longer just an organ, a piece of meat helping the school live and breathe. She existed on another plane from everyone else. She existed only to see Teacher. And the more she saw of Teacher, the more she wanted to keep seeing him.

But the ways in which she could see Teacher were limited. There was only so much she could see of Teacher by spying on him. To see more, she realized she had to use her imagination. She had to fill in the gaps. There were many gaps to fill. She filled them slowly and meticulously over the years and terms, filling in the answers in her mind like it was the longest test.

What kind of sports did he like to play?

She knew he played sports. She could tell just by looking at him, at his skin, at his body. Sometimes he would kick a *takraw* ball with the boys in the class. He kept it in the air longer than any of the boys. He must have been a *takraw* player.

Which color did he like best?

He had never said it before and the other students had never asked him—they didn't care to learn stuff like this. They didn't like him enough to want to know the little things. They didn't like him the way she liked him. She liked him more than anyone else.

She thought he would like blue. On Fridays when he didn't wear white, he wore blue.

Why did his smile look like a frown?

She had quickly, almost immediately developed a fixation on his mouth. Something about the way he smiled made her want to look inside it. He rarely opened his mouth wide enough for her to see in-side. In this way the inside of his mouth was more erotic to her than his private parts. It was a way inside him. But with the way he pinched his lips she nearly thought she'd never see inside him.

One day, however, in her second term of spying, she did see it. She saw it almost accidentally through her binoculars. He was alone in the teachers' office. He had a long free period that term. He had leaned back in his office chair and stretched his arms above his head. And then his lips parted. His jaw extended. He yawned the way one can only yawn when no one was watching. She saw the pink of his tongue, his gums, his inner cheeks. And then she saw what he sought to hide.

He had crooked teeth.

His bottom teeth were more crooked than his top. They looked jagged, sharp. They weren't terribly crooked, not enough to merit fighting against every smile. But the fact he did fight against every smile because of it was terribly endearing.

She sat there in the fields with her binoculars still plastered to her face. Something flared up inside her. It felt like a frenzied panic, like she wanted to get up and run around screaming, but it was only excitement. She realized she had seen inside him. And she realized she knew something about him he didn't want anyone to know.

She felt so close to him.

She wanted to get closer.

What kind of women did he like?

The girls in his class liked him, but he didn't like them back. The girls sometimes asked him if he had a girlfriend, to which he would laugh and say he wouldn't tell them. He was too kind to break their hearts, she thought, and too moral to indulge them. The woman teachers liked him the same way the schoolgirls liked him. But he didn't like the woman teachers either. He was nice and polite to them, but he made no friends of them.

This one was tricky.

She had tried to imagine him with different kinds of women. But imagining him with women was one step away from imagining him with herself, and she never imagined him with herself.

She decided he liked men.

What kind of men did he like?

Older men. Stronger. Like the military men he taught about. Like warlords. Men who could really hurt him if they wanted to. Men who could hold him down.

What would he look like, being held down?

She was sixteen now. She thought about that kind of stuff a lot lately.

She decided that pain and pleasure expressed themselves similarly on the face. The people having sex on the TV always looked like they were hurting themselves. She knew what Teacher looked like when he was in pain now. To imagine him in bed was to imagine her hammer striking him.

She was glad to be able to think about these things without anyone knowing. Her thoughts were strictly internal, and no one would see them unless she wanted them to see them. She had no control of how people perceived her on the outside, but she had full control over her insides. She would let no one see her insides.

She took refuge inside herself. The questions about Teacher just kept coming, and she was eager, almost anxious to fill in every answer. He was the only subject she ever cared for and the only subject she was ever good at. And like a subject, she wasn't just seeing him, she was knowing him. She was understanding him. She was getting so close to him, and it was becoming a compulsion to get closer, to learn everything she could about him even if it meant creating parts of him herself. She could be close to him without ever having to speak to him. She could fall in love with him without ever having to form a relationship with him. She could put him inside her without ever having him touch her. All she had to do was convert him. And then he was no longer just her teacher. He was all the thoughts in her head.

But thoughts can only satisfy a girl for so long.

~

By the time she and her mother finished work, the medics were still trying to get the factory woman out of the machine. They had freed her head by cutting her hair, but they had opted to take the machine apart instead of amputating her hand at the wrist. They had to call in the fire department for machines that could cut through metal. It was more time consuming, more work. It was easier to cut through flesh than metal. But she supposed it was easier to put metal parts back together than flesh.

The factory woman had stopped making noises. She was lying in the machine and staring blankly when she and her mother passed by her again on their way out of the factory. The woman was not dead, just catatonic. There was an IV drip like a wire attached to her arm, evidently pumping pain killers into her. But that blank expression on the woman's face looked like boredom, and as she passed by the woman, she couldn't help but imagine even pain that immense could get old after a while.

~

The smell had gotten very bad.

She and her mother returned home from the fish factory, and at once her mother began making a lot of noise about the smell. Her mother stood on the couch now, aggressively fanning the air with a handheld bamboo fan. "I can't stand that smell anymore," her mother said. "What the hell is it?"

She had an idea of what it was.

It was kind of fun to not tell her mother what the smell was, to make her believe she was the only one who could smell it. It was like when she heard things her mother couldn't. Once a frog had gotten into the house and was croaking up a storm, but her mother insisted there was no such sound and no such frog. That had annoyed her. So it had been kind of fun making her smell things she thought no one else could smell.

It wasn't so fun right now. She wasn't in the mood to have fun right now.

Her mind felt fatigued and there was a gnawing in her stomach, almost like hunger, almost like her stomach was eating itself. She crept into bed. She buried herself in blankets and tried to sleep. She didn't want to be awake. She didn't want to think about the fact that when she next woke up, it would be Friday. The last day of the term.

"I'm about to throw up," she heard her mother say.

She poked her hand outside her blankets and reached under her mattress. She pulled out her blood-stained school shirt. It was difficult to get it out while she was on top of it. She had to yank on it. She nearly tore it. When she finally got it, she brought it under the blankets with her. The blood had dried brown at this point. It looked more like a shit stain than a blood stain. It had a slightly rough texture now. She rubbed her fingers into it, but no blood came off no matter how hard she rubbed. It was like he was trapped in fabric. It was like she couldn't reach him anymore. She brought the shirt to her face and sniffed it. She couldn't even catch a hint of the metal of his blood. She couldn't smell anything except the bad smell of the apartment.

She sighed. She squeezed her eyes shut. She put the shirt on her head and over her face like a mask, and she pulled it tight like she meant to suffocate herself, like it was a suicide bag. But she didn't want to be dead, she only wanted to be asleep.

She felt the air grow thin. She felt her head grow light. She felt her nerves tingle like static. She felt the rough patch of Teacher's blood-stain against her skin. She wanted to press Teacher closer to her, to conjure him up in her dreams. She wanted to enter a dreamworld where she didn't have to imagine things herself, where things were imagined for her. But the tighter she pulled the shirt, the louder her mother's noises became. It was like the shirt amplified the sound. It now sounded like a great bird was flapping its wings right in her ears. She was so confused she took the shirt off her head. It was then she realized the shirt wasn't making her mother louder. Her mother was only getting closer to her.

Begrudgingly, she poked her head out of the blankets. Her mother stood at the doorway, fanning the air violently, inadvertently propelling the stench toward her.

"I called the landlord," her mother informed her. She was red in the face from all her fanning. "He should be here any minute."

She thought of the landlord arriving on all fours like a bloodhound, sniffing up and down the apartment, trying to track the smell. She might have been tickled by such a thought, but it wasn't fun right now. When things weren't fun it was hard to imagine a time when they would be fun again. It seemed it would never be fun again.

She gathered her blankets and before she disappeared beneath them again, she said to her mother, "Tell him to check upstairs."

It was like pressing the mute button.

Her mother suddenly stopped her fanning. Then, she looked up at the ceiling and frowned in revelation.

~

It had been no obligation on her part to check on the old lady upstairs, but it certainly would have been a decent thing for a neighbor to do.

The old lady lived in the apartment above their own. It was the attic apartment, and the carpeted floors up there did nothing to absorb any sound. Down under, she heard everything. She could hear every floorboard creak, every slippered footfall, every scratch of the walker against the carpet, and every frustrated shriek the old lady was accustomed to emitting every now and again. It was in this way she almost felt close to the old lady.

Admittedly they had never spoken to one another, but she felt there was no need to when she already knew so much about the old lady. She knew what movies the old lady liked and what movies she turned off. She knew what music the old lady listened to and which songs she sang along to. She knew her habits, her daily routine. What time she rose from bed, what time she ventured to the kitchen for meals, even the time of her bowel movements—surprisingly regular.

She knew what made her laugh, what made her cry, what made her scream. Meanwhile the old lady knew not even her name. She liked it that way.

And so when the old lady's sounds suddenly stopped like a TV unplugged, the apartment was enveloped in silence. It was a strange silence. It was almost like a sound in itself. It was so thick, like cotton deep in her ears, she often turned on her own TV just to mask it. She knew the old lady must have been dead, but she hadn't said anything. The smell soon emanated through the vents and invaded their own apartment, and she still hadn't said anything.

~

The landlord arrived and, upon finding the old lady long dead and melting into the carpet, finally called for cleanup.

~

The campus was full of smoke like some war-torn village. But it was only grilled pork.

It was the last day of the term and the students were celebrating with *mu kratha*. They had little electric stoves all over campus. They were gathered in groups, grilling meat together. It was a very windy day, and the wind was making the smoke spread rapidly. The smoke was even beginning to fill the ventilation unit which she was currently curled up in.

It was making her cough, yet she couldn't bring herself to leave the vent. She couldn't even bring herself to peer through her binoculars. It was always hard for her on these last days, but today was the hardest it had ever been.

Her head rested against one wall of the vent. Her feet were propped up on the opposite wall. She had just acquired her yearbook, and she now had it in her hands. It was a flimsy thing, more dusty than glossy, like a cheap magazine. She flipped through it impatiently. The smoke was making her eyes sting now. She squinted through the smoke and turned pages until she reached the teachers' page. Quickly, she found Teacher. She thought she would find some solace in his teacher's portrait. But the sight of it only made her heart plummet.

He was so handsome in the portrait. Too handsome.

The photo had been heavily edited. Everything about him was altered in one way or another. Everything that made Teacher her teacher was distorted. It was him, but it wasn't him. His skin, which had always been tan, was so pale it nearly blended into the white background. His teeth, too, were pure white. He was smiling with his teeth. He never smiled with his teeth. His lips looked redder. His eyes looked bigger. He had been staring right at the camera when the picture was taken. Now it looked like he was staring right at her.

She slammed the book shut.

Today was the last day of the term. This photo would be all she would have of him until next term. But would this photo be enough to fulfill her until then when it didn't even really look like him?

She felt that bubbling feeling in her chest. The kind of frustration that ends in a burst. The kind she only ever felt before in math class.

She was reminded of a growing problem.

Recently, she realized, her imagination was getting weak. Its power was fading. She couldn't imagine Teacher as well as she used to. It was the strangest thing. The longer she knew him, the harder it was to conjure him up in her head. Perhaps she knew him too well. Perhaps he lived too long in her head. Perhaps her head was changing him. She didn't know. All she knew was that with each passing term she was beginning to feel further from him, and she only had so many terms left with him.

The feelings of frustration kept bubbling. It was hot in the vent, even hotter than usual with the *mu kratha* smoke. Her hair stuck to her face with sweat, and it was hard to breathe. She knew she should flip through the yearbook again, search for other photos of Teacher, ones where he wasn't edited into perfection, ones where he looked more like himself, but she couldn't bring herself to. She was convinced no photo could capture him the way he was to her. She was convinced no one, no camera, no eye could see him the way she could.

She heard laughter outside, loud and grating amid the sound of meat sizzling, and she wanted to cover her ears. Her frustration kept building, and just when she thought it would burst like it had burst once before in a math class, the laughter outside turned to familiar, joyful screams.

"Teacher!" young voices screamed.

It was like a button in her being pressed. Automatically, she poked her head out of the vent.

Teacher had made an appearance, and already her frustration began to melt.

He looked so much better in person.

He looked so young on Fridays. The teachers didn't have to wear their civil servant uniforms on Fridays. Today he wore a white button-up shirt, sweat-stained from the day. The stains turned some parts of the shirt translucent, other parts yellow. She could even see patches of his skin in the places where the fabric stuck to him. His green-brown skin. His real skin, not his yearbook skin.

Her eyes followed him desperately, almost hungrily. He had just emerged from the teachers' office and was trying to be discreet, but as soon as his students saw him they began trying to feed him furiously.

"Just one! Just one!" they said. They looked so little, these twelve-year-olds, and they only reminded her of how old she was, how much time had passed since she was one of them. Their laughter sounded like shrieks, and Teacher laughed his silent laugh as he tried to reject them. He pretended to run from them. He was making a fool of himself again. He would always make a fool of himself just to make kids laugh. He was so kind.

The small horde of twelve-year-olds wielding chopsticks with meat were now upon him. They chased him, grabbing him by the wrists until at last he allowed himself to be fed once. The students cheered.

"Delicious?" they said. "Delicious?"

"Delicious," he said, though he probably burned his mouth on it.

The students cheered again. The wind blew very hard. It blew Teacher's ungelled hair off his forehead. She could just barely see the little cut she had created, a slit of red among smooth, miraculously unbruised skin. Still chewing, Teacher waved at the students, and then he was on his way again. Had today been any other day she would have stumbled from her vent and followed him. Instead, she settled back into her vent.

She knew he wasn't going anywhere.

Today all teachers were required to stay until nightfall for a dinner party to celebrate the end of the term. These parties were held on the last day of every term. Teacher didn't like these parties, she knew. The other teachers bothered him a lot at these parties. The director bothered him even more than the other teachers did. But he had no choice but to attend. She was going to attend, too. She always spied upon these end-of-term parties. They were her own way of saying goodbye to Teacher, to get one last look at him to satiate her for the two months until the next term.

As she curled back into her vent, she feared nothing could satiate her anymore.

~

She had a very bad, very white dream. The whole dream was painfully white, like staring straight into hospital lights. But she wasn't in a hospital, she was in the yearbook. Teacher was there with his yearbook face, his yearbook skin, emitting a type of brightness that made her squint even in her dream. A type of brightness not just overwhelming, not just terrifying, but dangerous. A type of brightness that could render someone blind.

When she woke up, she woke up blind.

The white of her dream was suddenly gone. It had turned into a darkness so black it was nothing, so black she couldn't tell if her eyes were open or not. She couldn't even tell if she had eyelids to open. She couldn't tell if she had a body. She must have had a body because, while she couldn't see, she could feel herself sweating, burning. She could feel her lungs suffocating. The only air there was to breathe was thick, sticky air that smelled like pork.

She suddenly remembered the *mu kratha*. And then she remembered she was in her vent. She remembered the teachers' party.

She flailed her limbs in a panic and struggled to get out of the vent. She couldn't tell which way was up or down. She was light-headed, and her temples throbbed from the suffocating sleep and the bright nightmare. She fumbled about, striking her elbows and knees against the metal walls of the vent until she found the opening and stumbled out. She felt the air become a bit cooler, a bit more open, but she still couldn't see. Her eyes weren't adjusting. She felt the panic from the nightmare become the panic of having gone blind. She thought the smoke had eaten her eyes, the heat had melted them in their sockets. But as she whirled around in the darkness, she realized she still had eyes to see with when she saw something bright and white in the distance.

It was the canteen. The teachers' party.

Dazed, she grabbed her backpack and went to the lights. She didn't feel real. She felt like she was still in her terrible dream. Her head was heavy and her mouth was bad-tasting. Her clothes stuck to her with sweat and humidity. She didn't know what time it was. She didn't know how long the teachers' party had been going on for or how much time there was left of it. She began to run for it.

The canteen and its lights were getting bigger, stronger. Soon, she heard its noise. It was the noise of many drunken voices and of laughter swelling and fading. The party wasn't over yet. From the way it sounded, it must have been going on for hours, and it wasn't ending any time soon. It sounded like the roar of a machine.

She kept running toward it like she was running for her life. She was unsteady and teetering on her feet, and when she reached the nearest long grass fields she fell onto her bottom in the dirt. She burrowed herself among the grass leaves. She searched in her backpack for her binoculars. She found them and brought them to her face with such urgency she smacked herself with them. The tender skin around her eyes throbbed from the impact, but the pain was secondary to her desperation to find Teacher.

She peered through the lenses. They were hazy not from the air around her but from her own sweat, her own body heat. Through the binoculars, the canteen was bright like a stage. The scene that played out atop it was chaos. These parties were always dizzying, but this one made her motion sick. It was a swirl of lights and colors, sweat and mosquitoes, alcohol spilled and swallowed. Movement, too much to follow. Noise, loud enough to hear from where she was crouched. She searched for Teacher, but the teachers were packed and moving together like water. She couldn't find him, and a terrible thought dawned upon her and made her hands shake. The thought that Teacher had left early. That he wasn't here at all.

Her blurry lenses would only focus on red-faced teachers, laughing and talking and eating and drinking. She felt drunk just by watching them. Her head spun as she searched through them, between them, trying to find any trace of Teacher. But her hands shook too hard to see anything for more than a second.

Suddenly the binoculars were filled with a scary sight. It looked like a clown. It made her flinch, and her flinch made the grass leaves rustle around her, which made her flinch again. But it wasn't a clown she was seeing. It was only the director, an older woman whose makeup tonight was thick like cracked paint and running with sweat. She had had too much to drink because she was wailing instead of speaking. In one hand she clutched a lipstick-stained glass. Her other hand was low on someone's back.

Her breath caught. She knew it was Teacher's back.

She jerked her binoculars upward. She had jerked too hard, too desperately, and she only caught a flash of Teacher's face before she lost him again. But that flash made her insides rupture with affection.

She saw so much in just that flash—her eyes were trained to suck up and devour any small piece of him. She saw sobriety on his face.

CUTE AGGRESSION

Teacher didn't drink. She saw the discomfort on his face. He didn't like the director's hand on his back. He didn't like the other teachers swarming him either.

They formed a crowd around him, now blocking her view. They were all drunk and bothering him. They liked him a lot. They liked him the way the students liked him, but they seemed to like him best when he was uncomfortable. The director especially liked him when he was uncomfortable.

She tried hard to find Teacher again, but she could only see him for seconds at a time before she lost him in the crowd. It was an endless cycle of finding him, then losing him, then finding him again. It was maddening. It made her squirm in the grass field. It made the leaves rustle around her. Every small glimpse only made her more desperate, more frustrated. It was like drops of water on a parched tongue. She needed more than drops. She needed a mouthful.

She soon learned she could find Teacher by finding the director first. She couldn't see Teacher without also seeing the director. The director's hand was attached to his lower back. Her arm was ropy like an umbilical cord. She was old enough to be his mother. Teacher was trying to move away from her. He must have been trying all night because he was sweating and worn out and drained, yet the teachers around him were getting more excited and more inebriated by the second. They were closing him in without realizing it or without caring. They were keeping him put. They were trapping him. They were pinning him against the director. They were swelling like a storm around him, getting louder and louder. It felt like something was about to pop, to burst. And then it did burst.

She saw it in flashes through her binoculars. She couldn't have missed it.

The director's hand was no longer on his back but on his neck, not to choke him but to pull him. She pulled him right to her, and together they looked like a mother and son until she pulled him even closer. Until she kissed him. She kissed him on the mouth in front of the whole canteen, and Teacher was so shocked, he apologized. She didn't need to hear him. She saw the apology on his lips. Everyone roared with laughter. His lips, tinted by the director's lipstick, tried and failed to smile. A man teacher, just as drunk as the director, screamed, joking that he wanted one too. He puckered his lips and jutted his face into Teacher's face, and Teacher flinched away like a child about to be struck. Everyone laughed even more, even harder.

Floating above their laughter was the director's shrill voice, even more shrill when she was drunk, shrieking, "He's mine!" in a tone either joking or completely serious. Someone's hand came down to pet Teacher's head like a dog's. Another came to pinch his cheek. Another to pat his back. They loved to touch him. They loved to laugh at him. They must have thought he was cute when he was uncomfortable. They were more aggressive than the twelve-year-olds from before, the ones who had grabbed him by the wrists and shoved chopsticks into his mouth. They were bigger too. They made Teacher look not just small, not just delicate, but degraded.

She had never seen him degraded before.

It was a part of him she was seeing for the first time with her own eyes. And there were so many parts of him she had yet to see, she realized. She'd only ever imagined these parts before. But she was tired of piecing everything together herself. She was sick of imagining. She was bad at it and getting worse. She was sixteen now. She was too old for just pretending.

Her chin felt wet, and she realized her mouth was leaking. A pool had been forming. She hadn't even noticed. She was too fixated on him, too filled with affection and despair. He was cute even when he was unhappy, even when he was harassed. She felt pain in her palms. She tasted blood on her tongue. It was that aggression again. That urge to squeeze. That need to bite. Her insides felt like they had roped themselves into knots so tight she couldn't move, couldn't breathe. She wouldn't be able to handle another two months without seeing him, she knew. It wasn't enough to imagine him. It wasn't enough to draw him. It wasn't enough to look at pictures of him. It would be better to have him.

If only she could have him in a place where she could always have him, she thought. If only that hammer could have rendered him unconscious so she could have taken him to that place, wherever it was. Some place where she could just look at him and not have to conjure him. Some place where she could see him, the real him, with her own eyes. Some place where he could never leave her sight.

The crowd of teachers around Teacher was too dense, too fluid. She lost sight of him again. But this time, no matter how hard she searched, she couldn't find him. He wasn't resurfacing. It was like they had swallowed him up.

In a panic, she tore the binoculars from her own face and searched with her bare eyes. She saw him almost at once. She felt not relief, but terror.

He was at the edge of the canteen now. He had already grabbed his bag. It was slung over his shoulder. He slipped out of the canteen now. He was making his escape.

He was leaving.

Had he not been able to bear it any longer? Had the director's kiss been so awful he needed to leave? Had it been so bad he wouldn't come back at all? Not even next term?

He moved away from the canteen with no hesitation in his step, and she felt a compulsion like fire flourishing through her body, burning her from the inside, making her move. He was walking so fast, and he wasn't looking back. He was disappearing into the night, and her body moved for her like it had moved for her once before.

She scrambled to shove her binoculars into her backpack. She threw her backpack onto her shoulders, and her hammer slammed against her back, knocking the wind from her. He was already so far away. She had to run or else she'd lose him. And as she ran her backpack swung and the hammer hit her hard in the back with every step. She kept running despite the bruise she knew was forming. She couldn't see him anymore, but she knew where he was going. He was going to his motorbike. He was going to get onto that bike and drive away and never come back.

She ran to where she knew his bike was. He parked it in the same place every day, a lonely place, away from other motorbikes. She watched him so many times on that bike. It was a battered thing, but he loved his bike, and she loved it for how he looked on it, not when driving it but when lounging upon it. He would straddle it backward and lie atop the seat on his stomach to rest. He would look just like a woman.

She saw his bike emerge out of the darkness, and then she saw him. She stopped running, and her hammer gave her one last punch to the back. He straddled his bike now, forward not backward. She always hated to see him forward on that bike. It meant he was leaving. And he was really leaving now. He was going to leave and never come back and she couldn't even chase after him. She wasn't as fast as a motorbike. Her heart sank down to her stomach. She felt the urge to run to him, to slash his tires with her teeth, to chew through the wires, to bite a hole in his gas tank and leave him stranded here with her. She heard the restless jingle of his keys. She heard the engine begin to start. She thought she'd hear it roar to life, and she thought she'd scream along with it.

But it didn't start.

It would not start. It only stuttered. It only choked. It was breaking down like some divine intervention, like when she was placed in his class four years ago, like a miracle.

It was like she had made his bike break down just by imagining it.

Perhaps her imagination wasn't weakening. Perhaps it was only changing, evolving. Perhaps it was tearing its way out of her head and into the real world.

Her mind was so strong, it was keeping him here.

He kept trying to start the bike, but it just kept stuttering. She heard him say something then. It sounded like a curse. It couldn't have been a curse. Teacher never cursed.

He hopped off his bike. He was abandoning it. He began walking again, his stride as fast and determined as before. He walked toward the school exit. He was leaving on foot.

Did he live close enough to walk home? Or was he going to find a payphone? A bus stop? A mechanic's shop? A gas station? She didn't know, and she didn't care. She only followed him right out of the school.

She had never followed him out of the school before, but she felt no fear of being seen, only fear of losing him. She followed him down the *soi* along the grass fields. There was no one around, only she and Teacher. In the dark, it was like they were the only two people in the world. She could barely see him, but she could hear him, his footsteps never faltering, like he was never going back. She would never go back either. She would never go anywhere he wasn't.

They were reaching the end of the *soi* now. They approached the shopping district. There were only two shops with lights on. The 7-Eleven and the tropical fish store. They were far away, but they provided enough light to see Teacher's silhouette. When she did, it was almost like she had made him materialize out of the darkness. Like he had been plucked right out of her mind.

She quickened her step, if only to get closer to him, to make his silhouette even bigger.

The tropical fish shop, the brightest thing on the street, was straight ahead of them. There were so many lights in this shop, lights shining on the fish put in tanks and bags just to be looked at, their colored fins flowing like ink in the water and coloring the lights shining on them. She could see his silhouette even clearer amid these lights. He made the most perfect, most beautiful shadow.

Her insides ached. Her palms hurt. Her tongue bled.

She couldn't help herself anymore.

"Teacher!" she cried out. She nearly shrieked it. She wasn't a girl who shrieked.

He jumped as though startled, then he stopped and turned to look at her. She couldn't see his face in the darkness. She knew he couldn't see her face either. She was just a shadow to him too, and she just kept running toward him, so overcome by a compulsion to be close to him, like the desire to dig one's fingers into ripe soil.

She loved him so much she retreated inside herself. She loved him so much she changed him, and now he was so much more than her teacher. He taught history, and in her head he was every warlord he taught about, every prince, every peasant. Every aggressor, every victim, every executed man. He told stories of war crimes, of men tortured to death, and in her head he had been those men. Debased, defiled, pinned to the ground with a boot, beheaded with a dull blade while he was still alive. He could be anything she wanted him to be. She could have him do anything she wanted him to do, and she didn't even have to be involved herself. She didn't have to be a person anymore. She could be an eye always trained on him, an eye with no body, and now he was before her and she was still just an eye. Eyes were like hands, and she could touch him all she wanted, and it didn't matter if he felt anything. He was here just to be touched, just to be watched, and she was here not at all. He was close enough to touch now. She reached out and passed a hand over his waist, and he was taken aback. Just like at the canteen when he was kissed by the director, he had the same expression, and he looked to have the same compulsion to apologize. But it wasn't enough to touch, she wanted to squeeze. She reached out again and squeezed his side, to which he batted her arm away, but the squeezing wasn't enough, just like the touching wasn't enough. That hadn't satiated the feeling at all. He was slipping away from her. He pushed her away. She dropped and clung to his legs. She held fast to his legs. He pushed her again, just hard enough to make her stumble when he could have sent her flying. He had always been kind. And while she regained her footing, he hurried away from her like he had hurried away from the canteen. She still wanted to dig her fingers into his sides, claw at the skin, through the skin like soil, like fish parts. She wanted to have him, to keep him here now that he was here. She wanted him in a place where she could always see him. She wanted him in ways she never had him before.

She took her hammer from her backpack, and she bashed his head open.

PART II

THE HEAD BLEEDS MORE THAN anything.

She struck him hard with the first hit, so hard he stumbled to his knees, so hard he gasped and groaned at the same time. He flailed his arms and folded them over his head as though to protect himself. But it seemed the pain had disoriented him, perhaps blinded him, and he couldn't protect himself against blows he couldn't see.

She kept on hitting him.

She feared a repeat of that time in his classroom. She feared he would get back up and take the hammer from her all over again. But he didn't take the hammer from her. He didn't even try. He just covered his head. He just sat there on his knees. It was almost like he was allowing himself to be beaten.

She didn't stop hitting him.

She bashed his head over and over. She swung the hammer high and brought it down hard until his arms fell, then his body. And even when he was down, even when he lay there unmoving on the ground, she still didn't stop hitting him. She only wanted to make sure he would stay down. But amid her blows she suddenly realized she might be killing him.

She certainly could have killed him, hitting him like this.

Cold panic paralyzed her. She stopped striking him, and the abrupt halt of movement made the hammer slip from her grip and clatter against the concrete. She stared down at him. He looked like a shape on the ground, a shadow. He was still as a corpse, and shiny with liquid reflecting the distant lights from the fish shop. She knew the liquid must have been blood. She could smell it.

The familiar, metallic smell filled her, then kicked her.

It kicked her back into motion. She felt a jolt of panic, and she dropped down next to him. She took his throat into her hands. She tried feeling for a pulse but couldn't feel anything other than her own wild pulse in her fingertips. She gripped his throat tighter. She might have been strangling him. She was digging for a pulse now. She was desperate. The panic spread and only made her heartbeat quicker, louder. But then, above her own frenzy, she heard something. She couldn't tell what it was at first. She held her breath to hear it better.

Teacher was making noises.

They were wet little noises, like he was snoring. It confused her. She had never heard him make noises like that before. She almost doubted the sound came from him, but it could not have come from anywhere else.

If he was snoring, then he was breathing. If he was breathing, then he was alive. She hadn't killed him.

She felt a rush of relief so strong she had to sigh it out. And in her relief it suddenly occurred to her she was touching him.

His throat was still in her hands. His flesh under her fingertips. Teacher's flesh. It was Teacher she was touching. Her teacher. His body was still warm, still breathing, still his, yet he couldn't feel a thing. He was unconscious, but not dead, and she could touch him all she wanted now.

She retracted her hands from him in surprise.

She had done it, she realized. She had acquired him.

She paused. Then she laughed. A short, incredulous laugh. And then, like a child overwhelmed with choices in a candy shop, she did nothing.

She supposed she couldn't do anything until she moved him.

~

She prepared herself to drag him. She stood up and grabbed hold of Teacher's arms. They were heavy and limp. She wrapped her fingers around his wrists. His skin felt so malleable in her hands. She thought she would squish him like clay. But beneath the skin she could feel the stability of bone, a promise he would keep his shape. She squeezed his wrists hard. Then she gave him a tug.

He didn't move.

Not even an inch.

It surprised her. She nearly thought he was stuck on something, but there was nothing for him to be stuck on. It was only that she hadn't pulled hard enough. She would have to pull much harder if she wanted to move him.

She readjusted her grip on his wrists. She squeezed hard enough to leave finger marks on him, then she tugged using all her strength. She dug her heels into the concrete and tugged so hard her shoulders felt like they were being pulled from their sockets.

He moved maybe an inch.

She dropped his arms. They sounded like meat, slapping the concrete. She was already panting and sweating. Her heart was already hammering. The panic swirled in her stomach again. She knew she could carry heavy things. She had been working at the fish factory for a year now. She carried fish parts all the time. But Teacher was heavier than anything she'd ever carried before. How could he be so heavy? How was she to move him? It wasn't impossible to move him, but it would take all night. It would take all she had.

She whipped her head around. She searched wildly for anything that would help her. Down the street she could just make out the flower shop in the darkness. Now closed for the night, it would have looked like nothing more than a streetside garage if it weren't for the flatbed cart of discounted flowers parked outside its shut door.

She ran toward it.

She grabbed the flatbed cart and dumped the flowers onto the sidewalk. They fell apart easily. Their petals scattered all over the concrete and melted in puddles. She ran some petals over as she pushed the empty cart to where Teacher lay bleeding and snoring.

The cart was low to the ground, but she still struggled to get him onto it. She tried lifting him like a baby or a bride, but he was far too big for that. She tried to drag him onto the flatbed, but the wheels kept turning, the cart kept moving. Eventually she managed to get him onto the cart by moving him in pieces. Limb by limb, she put parts of him on the flatbed. A leg first, then an arm, then his head, and the rest of him followed almost naturally.

There wasn't a lot of room on the cart. She had to situate him in a tight fetal position. When he looked to be settled, she gave the cart a tentative push. He was still heavy. It was hard to push him. The cart's wheels were rusted over and crooked, and it was hard to steer straight. But the cart was moving, so she kept going.

She pushed the cart down the street through the empty shopping district, toward her apartment. She pushed hard and moved fast. Although it was dark and there was no one around to see her, the cart made a rattling noise as she pushed it. It made her nervous. She tried to move faster, but it seemed she was pushing the cart too fast, faster than it was meant to be pushed. It felt like the wheels of the cart were catching, scraping. She turned her head and looked down at the wheels. It wasn't the wheels scraping. Teacher's head was dragging on the ground as she pushed him.

He was leaving streaks of blood all over the sidewalk. She stifled a panicked noise. She stopped pushing and hastily tucked his head back into the cart. She had to bend his neck at an awkward angle to keep it in the cart. She looked at the trails of blood he had left behind. Instead of trying to clean them, she grabbed the cart and kept moving toward her apartment. She could only hope the blood would be gone by the morning. Evaporated or soaked up by the concrete. Maybe her mind could erase it.

~

The cart was too bulky to fit through the doorway of the apartment building. She struggled to tip the cart over. She dumped Teacher's body inside the apartment lobby. Then she gave the empty cart a great push down the sidewalk. It was much lighter without Teacher on it, and it drifted far away.

She stepped over Teacher to get into the apartment. She looked up at the first flight of stairs and couldn't fathom the trek she would have to make. She was tired just looking at it. She was so tired she could barely stand. Her whole body was wet. Her school uniform was plastered to her body with sweat. She needed a break.

She sat on the floor next to Teacher and leaned her back against the nearest wall. It was stained with piss, but it felt good to lean on. Teacher, on the floor, was still making those weird, snoring noises. They made her cringe. They almost sounded gross, but in a way she was grateful for them because they told her he was still alive.

She looked at him now under the yellow lighting of the lobby. It was the first time seeing him under direct light, and she was surprised, almost scared to see how drenched his head was in blood.

She couldn't make out any of his features. All she saw was red, like someone had taken a brush and painted him with it.

The blood still poured. It came out in gushes from his forehead. His forehead looked like one big, gaping wound. Gaping like a mouth, or like something else. She was about to reach out and wipe the blood from his face so she could see him better. But there was an abrupt, loud noise.

The creaking of a nearby door.

She jumped. She looked up and saw the drunk man who lived on the ground floor exiting his apartment. She felt a violent urge to flee, another urge to pee, but she forced herself to remain next to Teacher's body. She positioned herself so she covered Teacher's bleeding head from the drunk man's sight. The drunk man paused when he saw them on the floor. Bleary eyed and swaying where he stood, he stared down at them.

There was a stretch of silence.

She said as evenly as she could, "He's passed out drunk."

And the drunk man, perhaps relating, only grunted and nodded.

He maneuvered around them to exit the apartment. He had to step over them to do so, and she contorted her own body to make sure she covered Teacher's bashed head the entire time. There was no relief when the drunk man left. She knew he would be back in a few minutes. He only ever left the apartment to go to the 7-Eleven and back.

She gritted her teeth and reached for Teacher. She held him tightly to her, his back flush against her front. She wrapped her arms under his armpits and locked them over his chest. It was an embrace. It was so different from their last embrace. This one was much better.

He felt heavier than he had felt before. But she seemed to muster strength from Teacher in her arms. She was holding him, hugging him, feeling him, and he felt nothing. It was invigorating. It was a reminder she had him, and she'd better move him if she wanted to keep having him. Together, moving as one, she dug the worn heels of her school shoes into the grooves of the floorboards and pushed. Each push only propelled them an inch, but she kept pushing and scooting on her bottom until they reached the stairs. Then, she worked to scoot up the flight of stairs in the same manner. One step at a time.

It seemed an impossible feat. It felt like her arms would fall off. It felt like Teacher's weight would drag both of them back down the stairs. It was hard to breathe with Teacher against her like this. It was almost like he was crushing her. But somehow they were moving. They were making their way up the stairs. It was like her mind gave her strength her body didn't have.

They reached the top of the stairs. Her head rushed. Her body shook. She gasped for breath. They were outside her apartment now. She heard through the walls the sound of her mother's snoring mixed with the blare of the TV. Her mother must have fallen asleep on the couch while watching her nightly *lakorn*s. Her mother did this every night.

She reached a hand up to the doorknob, but then she froze.

Where would she put him?

She had nowhere to put him where her mother wouldn't see him. The only place where her mother never checked was under her mattress, and she couldn't fit Teacher under her mattress.

She couldn't bring him into her apartment, she realized.

At a loss, she looked around, hoping to find something that would help her again. There was not much. The hallway was small and tight. There was barely enough room for her and Teacher to lie. She looked down the flight of stairs they had just climbed. She couldn't bring herself to go back down after coming all the way up. She turned her head the other direction. She looked up the stairwell leading to the old lady's attic apartment.

At the top of the stairwell, the door was open a crack.

The sight of it was like cold water poured on a sleeper.

She felt herself jolt. She nearly thought the exhaustion was making her see things. But the crack was there just as Teacher was here. The cleaners who had come to take away the old lady's body must have left the door open.

It was another miracle.

It was her mind making things real.

She squeezed Teacher to her chest again.

The stairwell to the attic was narrow and steep, almost like a ladder. The cleaners couldn't even get their cleaning machines up the stairwell—she had heard their struggle through the walls yesterday. The old lady herself had rarely left her apartment because of those stairs. Toward the end, she left not at all. The climb had one day proven too treacherous, as evidenced by one particular shrieking session that had ended with the old lady screaming, despairing, *"Won't someone help me down the stairs?"* No one had responded.

How long it took to climb those stairs with Teacher in her arms, she wasn't sure. She wasn't aware of time, only of the feeling of being crushed and suffocated, being pushed beyond exertion, yet still driven forward by some desperate force. She wondered if this was what it was like to drown.

She moved the whole time in a half-awake daze, pushing her body so hard her limbs felt like they were tearing. Teacher almost fell from her arms many times. The sweat and the blood made everything slick. Soon she was seeing colors. Her body tingled. Her nerves screamed. She was on the verge of losing consciousness, but she kept propelling with her legs and scooting up the stairs step by step. It seemed like there were endless steps. It seemed like there would be no end. It seemed like she really was drowning, until suddenly her back collided against something hard and flat. The door.

She would have gasped had Teacher not been crushing her.

She clutched Teacher to her with one arm, clawing at his shirt and even locking her legs around his middle to keep him from falling, and with her other arm she pushed the door all the way open. With the little strength she had left, she flung her body along with Teacher's body in through the doorway. She collapsed on the floor with him. She awkwardly kicked her legs at the door. As it shut, it pushed out the dirty yellow light from the hallway and they were enveloped in warm, stuffy darkness, like a blanket over their heads.

She might have lost consciousness.

~

There was a smell. It smelled like a bathroom. It reeked not of shit but of skin—years of exfoliated skin trapped in a shower drain. Beneath the skin smell, there was the sting of urine and the near sweetness of rot. It was so potent it was like she had eaten it. She expelled it out of her nose and mouth with a violent cough. She covered her nose with her hands, but her hands were sticky and somehow smelled even worse.

She rolled onto her stomach. She groaned as she did so. Her body felt weak and loose, like taffy having been stretched and pulled. She knew her muscles would be sore and hurting later. She looked around. It was dark. She couldn't see Teacher, but she could hear him next to her. He snored louder and wetter than before. It almost sounded like he was grinding his teeth. She reached a hand out to touch him, just to make sure he was really still there with her. Her hand touched something hot and slippery, like the inside of a mouth.

It gave her a start. She thought for a moment her hand really was inside his mouth, but she then felt something hairy.

She realized it must have been his head she was touching. The wound on his forehead was what felt like a mouth. The warmth of it was somehow comforting, grounding. It was a warmth that could only come from life. She found she didn't want to bring her hand away. She wanted to put it in deeper. She prodded the wound with her fingers, wanting to see how deep she would go, when suddenly her fingers came in contact with hard bone.

She snatched her hand away as though she had been burnt.

It felt just like a fish bone.

She shuddered. She wiped her hands on her skirt. She suddenly wanted to turn on the lights. She sat up. She felt along the wall for a light switch. She found it, fumbled with it, then the room was lit up.

The sudden light hurt her eyes. It had a yellow tint to it, like the hallway light. She winced and squinted through it. The first thing she looked at was Teacher on the floor before her. His face was still covered in blood. She still couldn't see his features well. Her eyes went straight to his forehead. In her prodding, it seemed she had pulled apart the torn edges of his wound. The white bone of his forehead was now poking out, gleaming in the yellow light. It looked just like a fish bone too.

She reached out and smoothed the torn flesh down, covering the bone from sight.

She looked around the room then, and for a moment she was terribly confused. She had never been in this apartment before, but she thought she knew it well. She had it all mapped out in her head, the layout pieced together through sounds and creaks in the floorboards, pieced together as though with echolocation. But it looked nothing like how she thought it would look. She nearly thought that this was the wrong place, that this couldn't be the old lady's apartment.

It was the stain on the floor that told her otherwise.

The old lady must have died on her way to get food. Her corpse stain was on the carpet near the kitchenette. It was a reddish-brown color, tapering off to a pale yellow at the edges. It was in the shape of the old lady's body, almost like her shadow lying on the floor with one arm outstretched. A single corpse fly, heavy with blood, was still sucking at the dried fluid stuck on the carpet. The silence of the apartment made it sound like the corpse fly was in her ear. She rubbed her ear as though it were.

She averted her eyes from the stain. It made her uncomfortable. It was like the old lady was still here despite dying. It was like she would always be here. That stain didn't look like one that could be scrubbed out.

She didn't want to keep Teacher in this room if that stain was there.

She looked at the other rooms. The apartment was very small and simple and had only three rooms: a living room with a kitchenette, a cramped bathroom, and a bedroom. To the left she could see the bathroom. It was too small for Teacher, and too smelly. To the right was the bedroom. Its door was left wide open. Some of the living room's yellow lighting spilled into it. She could just barely see inside.

It looked like a box. It was windowless, and it was empty save for a sleeping mat in the corner and a small box TV pushed against a wall. The blue flowered wallpaper was peeling, coming off in chunks from the wall. A thin piece of metal jutted from the ceiling in the middle of the room, meant to hang a chandelier perhaps, but now looking as crude as a meat hook.

She felt a tugging in her stomach.

She stood up.

It took a long time to drag Teacher to the bedroom. Though she pulled hard, he was hardly moving. It felt like he was pulling away from her, but it was only his dead weight and gravity working against her. She took his bag off his body, thinking he would be lighter without it. The difference was miniscule. She could feel her strength depleting. She had used so much energy getting him here. She didn't have much left. Despite her fatigue she moved hurriedly, filled with worry the last of her strength would be sapped and she would no longer be able to move him at all.

She worked to drag Teacher to the center of the bedroom, right under the chandelier hook. When she entered the room, she immediately felt a change in temperature. It was very hot in this room. It felt even more humid than it did outside. It was hard to breathe, and when she did breathe, all she smelled was urine.

The urine smell seemed to follow them. It smelled worse in this room. She thought it was the warmth of the room intensifying it. But the smell almost seemed to be coming from directly beneath her.

It brought forth a bad memory.

Her hands flew to her school skirt. She touched the fabric between her legs, thinking she peed herself. Sometimes when she got

CUTE AGGRESSION

overwhelmed, she peed herself, like that one bad time in math class. But as she felt her skirt, she found it was only wet with sweat. She nearly thought the urine smell was coming from her head, that it was seeping out of her mind just to taunt her, just to make her feel bad. But then she looked down at Teacher at her feet.

It was dark in the bedroom. There were no lights and no windows. Even with the living room light spilling in through the open door, she could only see the shape of Teacher. She squatted next to him. Timidly, she reached a hand out and touched the front of his pants. The fabric was warm and wet. Just to be sure, she brought her fingers to her nose and sniffed.

Her suspicions were confirmed. It was Teacher who had wet himself.

She frowned. She kept smelling her fingers because she couldn't believe it. The thought of Teacher urinating in his pants was an odd one. It was a thought she had never considered before. In all the ways she had imagined him, she had never once imagined him pissing himself. For a moment she didn't know what to do. She figured the only thing she could do was remove his pants.

She fumbled with the buttons of his pants. She couldn't see what she was doing, and she had never unbuttoned the pants of another person before. It was different from unbuttoning her own pants. She had to mirror her movements. It took a while to get the hang of it. When the pants finally came undone, she tried to pull them down but the urine made the fabric stick to his skin. She had to fight to peel them off him. It was like peeling a hard, unripe orange.

Eventually his pants came off. His underwear came off with them. They seemed to be adhered to each other. She managed to pull them down to his ankles. They got stuck there. She remembered she needed to remove his shoes too. She removed his shoes and his socks along with his pants and underwear. All of them were wet with urine. He had peed a lot.

The smell and feeling of urine made her feel bad. It wasn't her own, but it felt like it was. She figured everyone's urine was the same.

She shook her head so hard it hurt her neck. Her hair would have flown off her forehead had it not been plastered there with sweat. She had more work to do. She couldn't let herself be distracted now. She needed to keep working before he woke up. It didn't look like he would wake up anytime soon. Still, she found herself rushing.

She supposed he needed to be tied the way dogs needed to be

chained, the way birds needed to be caged. If not forever, then initially. She went to the old lady's closet, hoping to find scarves or clothes she could tear into strips to bind him with. But when she opened the closet, she found nothing but fishing supplies.

She frowned through her confusion. She pushed past the poles and came across a coil of heavy-duty fishing line. She held it close to her face and squinted at the label. It promised to hold up to four hundred pounds. The line looked so thin. She doubted it could hold that much weight.

Warily, she began unwinding it.

She went to Teacher on the floor. She squatted next to him again. She bound his wrists together above his head with the fishing line. She wrapped it tightly around one wrist and then the other, weaving it back and forth between his wrists in a figure-eight. She wound it perhaps too many times. She used practically half the coil.

She stood up then. She jumped toward the ceiling, trying to loop the rest of the coil through the hook of the chandelier hanger. Though the floor beneath her creaked with every jump, her body felt strangely light. It nearly felt like she was floating in the air. She figured it was only the absence of Teacher's weight on her making her feel like nothing at all. It took a few jumps before she managed to snag the line through the hook. She fed the line through the hook and grabbed the other end. Then she pulled on it hard.

Too hard.

The line slipped through her hands and sliced open her own palms. She inhaled so sharply her throat made a whistling sound. She swallowed the cry that tried to escape her mouth. The pain was hot. It felt like her palms were burning. Yet despite the pain and the blood she felt spilling from her hands, she gripped the line harder and continued to pull on it. She felt the line digging into her cuts, but she kept pulling. She was reeling him in and hauling him up like he was the biggest fish.

She tried to haul him upright, all the way to his feet, but he was far too heavy and she was far too spent. The furthest she could haul him was to his knees. She let him stay like that, hanging from the ceiling by his wrists and sitting on folded knees like a child.

His weight was still working against her, still feeling like he was pulling away from her, resisting her. It was like she was playing a game of tug-of-war with him, with rope that bites. Her body shook hard like she was cold, but she felt like she was burning. The line felt like hot metal in her palms. She struggled to tie her end of the line to the bars of the radiator on the wall in order to keep him propped up this way. Her hands were slick with her own blood, and just as the line was beginning to slip from her grip, she managed to secure it to the radiator. She promptly collapsed to the floor with her own effort. She felt a great release. The sudden absence of weight once again made it feel like she was floating when really she was pinned to the floor with exhaustion. The room was dark, but her swirling head made her see bright fuzz before her eyes, like TV static. Through this static, she looked at her own sliced hands. They stung terribly. They spouted so much blood. She clenched them into fists. She tried to regain her breath. She had been panting. It sounded like she was hyperventilating. She wiped sweat from her brow, smeared blood on her brow. Slowly, fatigued, she made her way from the floor to her knees, then from her knees to her feet despite the head rush threatening to knock her over again. She stood, despite everything, and looked at him.

Strung up like Saint Sebastian. Just like a saint.

~

She turned on the TV and muted its volume. She only wanted its light.

TVs were bright things, she knew. She used to watch TV constantly, and though she had stopped watching it after meeting Teacher, she still used hers as a nightlight sometimes. The TV in the old lady's bedroom was a small, boxy thing, set directly across from where Teacher was hanging, but its blue, glowy light was strong. It lit up almost the whole room, coloring it something new with every change of scene. She aimed it so it would shine right on Teacher. She could see him more clearly now.

As her eyes took him in, she was struck by an intense giddiness.

She had never felt such a thing before. She was so giddy she could have danced. She might have, had her body not been so worn out.

Teacher was displayed right before her, hanging there limply from the ceiling. His head was down, his face hidden, his chin touching his chest. His forehead still poured blood. His wrists, too, now bled. The fishing line cut into his skin. It cut into him like it had cut into her. The blood trailed slowly, steadily down his forearms. The TV light made it look more like chocolate syrup than blood, but it still smelled strongly of metal.

Teacher had stopped making those snoring noises since being pulled upright. He had become so quiet she would have thought him dead if it weren't for the faint quiver of breath moving his stomach beneath his shirt. His white shirt was now wrinkled and stained with blood and dirt. It was partially undone. Some of the buttons must have come off in the struggle to acquire him. She could see parts of his chest. The edges of the shirt looked like skin pulled apart during a surgery. Seeing underneath his shirt was like seeing inside him. She felt a pool in her mouth again. She wanted to dance again.

She went to him, nearly skipping as she did so. She knelt before him. She brought her hand to the bare skin of his chest. She pressed and felt his heart beat against her. It was almost like she had his heart in her hand. She felt so close to him. Her hand traced him downward, over the shirt now. Her hand was like an eye, and she saw his body through it. His body was that of a youth, just like she had imagined. As hard as it was soft. Her hand kept moving downward. The shirt was long and wrinkled, bunched up between his legs. It covered his penis.

She had spied on him in the bathroom so many times, but she had never seen his penis before.

Lingering beneath the giddiness was another feeling. It was uncomfortable, but she knew it was one of those good feelings that feel bad. Good feelings were always one step away from bad feelings. Sometimes it was impossible to tell the difference. Though his shirt covered him, she knew he was baring parts of himself she had never seen before. She was eager to see these hidden parts, and the eagerness felt more like anxiety. Her hand shook as it reached out and grabbed his shirt.

She lifted it up. She unveiled him.

The sight confused her. She was so confused she made a sound.

His penis was quite small. It didn't even touch the floor between his legs. A funny little thing, she thought. Just a piece of flesh dangling.

At sixteen she had an idea of what sex was like. She had never had it, but she had seen it before on the TV, and she had learned about it in school too. Even Teacher had mentioned it once in his class. He had very carefully brought up the topic of wartime rape. She had tried to imagine him raping and him being raped, and though she preferred the latter, it was hard to put it together in her head because there were so many missing parts. She had never seen a penis before. She had only heard about them. She didn't know what they looked like in reality. And when Teacher had told those stories of wartime rape, she

CUTE AGGRESSION

thought them to be strong and scary things, things that could do a lot of harm. But she looked at Teacher's penis now and it was just a little thing.

She couldn't understand how such a little thing could do so much harm. It would be so easy to cut off. Easier than fileting a fish. There weren't even any bones to work around.

She let go of the shirt. She looked down at his legs instead. The way they were folded was making the meat of his legs bulge. His skin looked even more pliable like this. It looked smooth and shiny, too, with the TV light reflecting off the urine still on his legs. Curiously, she touched his thigh. It was damp and soft, softer than his wrists, and almost spongy with muscle. She poked his thigh and watched his skin bend under the pressure of her fingers, only to bounce right back up as soon as she removed the pressure.

It felt right. It was like his legs were made to be squeezed. She felt another surge of giddiness. She poked the skin of his thigh again. She grabbed a fistful of it. And as she played with him as such, his leg suddenly twitched against her.

She flinched. She took her hand away.

It was only a small twitch, a brief quiver of muscle before he was still again. He made no more movements, no more signs of consciousness, but the twitch had really frightened her. She had forgotten he was ever capable of moving on his own.

She needed to make it so he couldn't move on his own.

She remembered his legs weren't tied, only his wrists were. He couldn't run away with his wrists attached to the fishing line, but he could stand up. Worse, he could kick.

She felt a sliver of unease. She considered what would happen when he woke up. She tried to imagine how it would go. She figured he might be scared and confused like he had been when she hit him the first time in his classroom. That time he had been so scared and confused he had stood up and gotten away from her.

The unease spread. She rose from her kneeling position and grabbed the coil of fishing line. She had used most of the line to string him up, but there was still some left. With a hunting knife she found among the fishing supplies in the closet she cut two separate lengths of line. She went to him again and wound each line around each folded leg, tying his left thigh to his left calf, his right thigh to his right calf. This way he wouldn't be able to unbend his legs to kick or stand. He would have to remain sitting there with his folded legs spread in a *V.*

She tied the line tightly. It dug into the elastic skin of his thighs. The skin puckered around the line and bulged even more. His legs looked like balloons being squeezed. They looked like they would burst. She thought she tied the line too tight. She considered cutting it and trying again. She nearly did.

It was then he woke up vomiting.

~

It nearly scared her right out of the room.

He convulsed suddenly, almost violently, and fluid spewed from his mouth. It got all over her shirt. She could feel it seeping in through the fabric, warm and wet, as she flinched hard. She fell backward, right onto her bottom, and as he continued to cough and sputter, she felt the urge to scramble away from him as though he were something dangerous.

His movements were jerking and harsh. He tried to double over and vomit, but his binds kept him put. Still, it seemed he couldn't stop vomiting. He gasped, trying to breathe between each retch, but he only inhaled the fluid his body was trying to eject. He coughed, choking on his own vomit, and suddenly the urge to go to him was stronger than the urge to get away from him. She found herself reaching out to him. She saw her own hands touching him on the shoulder and on the chin. She saw her uncertain fingers trying to reach inside him and clear his airway. But as soon as she touched him, he flinched violently as though frightened, as though he didn't know someone was there to touch him.

He made noises even stranger and uglier than his snoring from before. Noises like he was scared. He was thrashing now, too, trying to shake her off him. He thrashed so hard it was almost like he was flinging her hands from him. Like he was hurting her.

Shocked, she could only shrink away from him and watch as he continued to struggle.

He tugged at his wrists. He tried to unfold his legs. He realized he couldn't move, that he was bound, and then he yanked against his binds. All the while he still made those terrible, scared noises. He still gasped for breath. His mouth still leaked vomit.

He must have been confused. He must have been hurting in so many different places. She reached for him again. She had her hands on his shoulders. She said, "Teacher, it's okay!" But her voice couldn't be heard over the sounds he made, and her touch only made him wilder.

He bled even more now that his heart was racing. It came out of his forehead in rapid throbs. It got into his eyes. He probably couldn't see her. He probably didn't know it was just a girl who was touching him, not some monster or some killer. He thrashed even harder. He tried to rip himself free from his binds, but his struggling seemed to make his binds even tighter. The line bit into his flesh. It cut him so deep. It made blood spurt from his wrists and thighs, and now he cried out in pain. He yelped and whined just like a hurt dog. He was frightened, not like how a human is frightened, but like an animal.

He was being so loud. Every jolting movement he made caused the floorboards to scream. Her mother was right under them. Her mother couldn't hear most things, but he was being so loud she feared even a half deaf person would hear him. She tried to shush him, to make him still. But the noises he made still drowned out the sounds of her shushing.

"Teacher, *please*," she tried, but now she couldn't even hear herself.

She thought she would have to hit him in the head again, make him unconscious again just to quiet him. She tore her eyes from him and searched for her hammer. She couldn't find it. It wasn't here. She realized she hadn't brought it back with her. She must have left it on the street.

A new kind of panic exploded in her, and Teacher was getting louder and more violent by the second. He kept pulling hard at his wrists and his skin was splitting open. She could hear it squelching. The line squeezed him so tight it turned his hands purple. It looked like his hands would pop right off.

She lunged for the hunting knife on the floor. Her hands were wet with sweat and blood, and she gripped the knife hard to keep it from slipping. She went to him. She jabbed the blade at the fishing line around his wrists, only wanting to cut him down so he would stop hurting himself, so his hands wouldn't come off. But he moved too much, he thrashed too hard, and instead of cutting the line, the knife cut into one of his fingers.

She hadn't meant for it to cut him.

She certainly hadn't meant for it to cut the whole thing off.

But the knife was very sharp.

With the slightest bit of pressure, his index finger fell to the floor. She couldn't understand what happened at first. She felt her body freeze over in shock. She looked at his hand. She saw the stump. She looked at the floor. She saw the finger. It bounced a few times as it landed and settled against the carpet.

Teacher was louder now. His noises grew sharp and piercing and grating. It snapped her out of her paralysis. It made her hands fly to him again. She grabbed his hair nearest to his forehead, wanting to grab his attention, to make him listen to her, but when she lifted his head up, the wound on his forehead began to split even further. The force of her pulling and the force of his own struggle against her made the torn skin peel upward and pull away. He was being scalped.

He yelled even louder. He was even wilder, even more like an animal. She couldn't think when things were so loud, and she couldn't believe it was Teacher making those noises, and so she wasn't thinking when she aimed the hunting knife at the source of the noise. She inserted the blade inside his mouth. She dug it into the side of his tongue. She dug hard and he spilled blood.

The knife just disappeared into him.

He stopped screaming only because blood filled his throat.

His screams turned into gurgles. Then he began choking on the blood like he had choked on his vomit.

Startled, she pulled the knife out. She stumbled backward, falling onto her bottom again. Immediately he leaned forward as much as his binds would allow and sputtered. He attempted to spit out the blood choking him, but when he spat, along with the saliva and blood came half his tongue.

It dangled from his mouth, a hunk of meat. And for a moment he seemed confused, like he didn't know where this meat in his mouth came from. But it didn't fall to the floor when he spat it out. It remained there on his chin. He must have realized the meat was him and that it was still attached to him because he then sucked it back into his mouth as though on instinct, as though he didn't know what else to do, as though he scarcely knew it was his tongue hanging on his chin.

She ran out of the room. She could do nothing else.

~

She made it halfway down the attic stairs before her legs gave out. She fell onto her bottom once again. She felt a bruise forming there already. Had she not been clutching the railing she would have tumbled right down the stairs. But she caught herself, and then she remained frozen, sitting there on the stairs, still clinging to the railing like she was hanging off the side of a cliff.

She felt Teacher's cries in her hands. He cried so loud it vibrated through the railing.

She couldn't move. She couldn't even blink. If she closed her eyes even for a moment her mind would flood with images of Teacher's finger on the floor. His tongue dangling on his chin. The knife moving through him like butter. Parts coming off him so easily.

The flesh was more fragile than she thought. As fragile as any dead fish.

She thought of fish at the factory simply falling apart in her hands. And then she thought of that factory woman getting caught in the machine and falling apart just the same. That woman had been tangled so badly, yet the medics had chosen to take the machine apart instead of taking her hand off at the wrist. They must have known it was hard to put flesh back together.

She felt fear, cold in her stomach.

Teacher's cries vibrated up her arms like electric currents shocking her back to life, reanimating her. She scooted on her bottom all the way down the stairs with a new sense of desperate urgency. A bad smell followed her the whole way. It smelled like a mouth. Like a stomach. She had half a mind to remember Teacher had just vomited all over her shirt. He had woken up spewing parts of himself too.

When she reached the bottom of the stairs, she crawled all the way to her apartment on her hands and knees. She had no strength to stand, and she felt safer close to the ground like this, like a bug almost too small to exist. She reached an arm up and opened her apartment door. As soon as it opened, blue TV light spilled out into the hallway. Her mother was still asleep on the couch. The *lakorn* she had fallen asleep to was long over, replaced now by an infomercial for skin whitening products. It must have been very late at night, and with the way her mother was snoring, she must have been deeply asleep.

Evidently, she hadn't heard a thing.

Staring up at her sleeping mother, she felt like a child again. Whenever she had a nightmare as a child, she would wake her mother. She hadn't done such a thing in years. She had long since learned to keep her nightmares to herself. And the disturbance she now felt was one not even a mother could quell.

She rose from the floor. It took a long time. Her muscles felt loose and impotent. They had been sapped of all their strength. It was like they weren't even muscles anymore, just meat. She knew they would hurt later.

When she made it to her feet she walked past her mother. She walked through the living room to the sound of Teacher's cries above her. Her body was uneasy. Every step was unsteady. It felt like she was shivering, but she wasn't cold. She went to a closet where her mother kept a box full of sewing supplies. Her fingers were stiff as they plucked out a needle and a spool of thread. The needle was large and the thread was coarse and black. She put them in the pocket of her school skirt. They would have to do.

~

Walking back into the attic was like walking into a rancid mouth. It smelled like how her shirt smelled. The smell enveloped her. The sound of Teacher's cries filled her ears like water. She would have more readily believed it was an animal crying inside that room, not Teacher. It sounded nothing like him. It sounded ugly and scarcely human. It sounded wet, too, and she knew he was bleeding from the mouth he cried from. The mouth his tongue had been dangling from.

She felt the needle in her pocket poking at her, urging her toward him. But she stopped short of entering the bedroom. Her heartbeat throbbed slowly like a toothache, painful in her chest. She found herself unable to step inside.

Everything was different now that he was awake.

He cried so much he must have cried the blood right out of his eyes. He would see her if she walked in that room.

And what would he see of her?

She waited for the TV in the bedroom to get dark. She knew it had to get dark eventually. There had to be a pause between program and commercial. It would only last a few seconds, but that was all she needed.

Soon the TV did dim, the room did darken, and she dashed in on the tips of her toes. She tried to be silent, but the floorboards in the attic creaked loudly under her steps, and Teacher made a startled noise in his throat, disrupting his wet crying. By the time the TV regained its light, she was behind him, but Teacher knew she was there.

He started breathing hard, gasping as though frightened. He tried to look at her, but with the way he was strung up, it was hard for him to turn around. Even if he craned his neck, his own raised arms blocked his line of view. Not being able to see her seemed to frighten him even more. His gasping turned into hyperventilation. She could see the blood gushing from his cut finger in rapid bursts, in time with his quickening heartbeat. It gushed from his forehead in the same manner.

He stopped trying to crane his neck to see her. He looked up at his wrists instead, and he tried once more to wring them loose from the fishing line. He looked like a child trying to wring its hand from its mother's grip. And like a mother's grip, the fishing line only tightened around his wrists the more he pulled.

The fishing line was a terrible mistake, she realized.

It cut into his skin, turning his wrists into messes of torn flesh. A surge of disgust and panic sent her hands flying out toward him. She grabbed his wrists to stop him from cutting himself further. He recoiled as soon as she touched him. He choked on his own breath and stopped his wringing. He became stiff. It was like he had hardened under her hands. Even his skin turned rigid. It was not at all like the pliant skin she had felt before. It would have felt like corpse skin had it not been for the hot blood she felt gushing into her hands to the beat of his alive heart.

Her eyes trailed downward. She looked at his upturned head, tilted up so far she could see the gaping wound on his forehead. She saw him looking right at her hands on his wrists.

She let go of him. She nearly flung her hands from him.

He remained stiff even when she was no longer touching him. The only thing moving him was his uneasy breath. He still looked up at his wrists as though he could still see her hands on him.

Frantically, she looked at her own hands to see what he had seen. They dripped with blood, his and hers. They were obviously a girl's hands, small with stubby fingers and bitten nails. He must now know it was a girl standing behind him.

Her mouth went dry. Too dry to swallow.

She wiped the blood from her hands on her school skirt. Then quickly, rashly, she reached her hands out to him again. She gripped the fabric of one of his shirt sleeves. She felt his arm tense against her, hardening. His eyes latched onto her hands again. He looked at her hands on him, then the wrists attached to those hands, then the arms. She felt her skin prickle into gooseflesh. She wondered if he could see the bumps.

She yanked hard at the fabric, tearing a long strip out of his sleeve, and Teacher made a noise like she was tearing his skin. She moved her hands and the torn fabric in them away where he could no longer look at them. The fabric was so thin it was practically see-through, and she remembered looking at his skin through it only a few hours earlier at school. It seemed like a lifetime ago. Things had changed so much since then. It seemed like another life entirely.

She folded the strip of fabric to make it thicker and opaque. Then she reached forward and wrapped it around his eyes like a blindfold. She thought he would thrash against her, shake his head, and make things hard for her, but he didn't even resist. He only grew more stiff, like a mannequin.

She tied the makeshift blindfold in a knot at the back of his head. Then she backed away from him. She rubbed her hands on her arms as though to wipe the feeling of his eyes from her skin. She rubbed until the bumps went away, and then she kept rubbing.

Slowly, she ventured out from behind him. She had to make herself. Her feet felt glued to the ground. She could only move centimeters at a time. She inched her way to his front, moving slowly and testing each step before setting her foot down to keep the floorboards from creaking. She stood before him, and he didn't lift his head to meet her gaze. He didn't know she was in front of him at all.

It was only when she sighed in relief that he jerked his head in her direction.

Though he couldn't see her, it gave her a start. She took a flinching step backward and the floorboards creaked. His head jerked again. He beared his blindfolded face to her. It was almost like he was looking at her. She had to stifle the urge to run. She had to tell herself he wasn't looking at her, that he couldn't see out of his eyes right now. He couldn't see a thing.

She stood before him, still like a mannequin too. She feared any movement would make a sound he would hear, and those sounds would be pieced together in his mind to create an image. She feared even her own breath would be audible. She remained frozen, holding her limbs close to her body, breathing shallowly until her lungs burned. She did nothing but look at him. She watched his forehead wound throb like a heart. She watched blood gush from it and stain the blindfold red. She watched blood pour from his lips in strings. She watched blood burst from the stump where his finger used to be.

So much of him was leaking out. So many holes had been made in him.

She reached forward and grabbed hold of his other shirt sleeve. Teacher's own breath hitched and he tilted his chin in the direction of her hand. He couldn't see her hands, but he could still feel them on him. She quickly tore a second, smaller strip off the shirt sleeve.

With the fabric she tried to wrap up the bloody stump where his finger had been, but as soon as the fabric touched the stump, Teacher cried out louder than before. He cried so hard his tongue flopped out onto his chin again. He sounded like a yelping animal, unaware of how ugly it sounded, and she backed away from him in fright. She saw even more blood gushing from the stump, shooting straight up at the ceiling like a fountain.

She figured the exposed nerve endings must have been sensitive. When parts were cut off, it must have made the remaining parts even more alive. Merely touching him there must have hurt worse than the actual severing of the finger.

She tried something else. She wrapped the strip of fabric around his finger instead, below where the cut was, avoiding the nerve endings altogether. She tied it tight with a knot like a shoelace, and the pressure of it made bone and meat spill out of the stump. It reminded her of squeezing claws out of a cat's paw.

Teacher groaned all the while and his face beneath the blindfold contorted, but he wasn't yelping like an animal anymore. She finished tying the knot. It looked like a bow around his finger, but it proved to be a decent tourniquet. The blood stopped spurting out of his finger. It only oozed now, dripping downward and soaking into the fabric of the blindfold.

Teacher wriggled his finger. She wondered if he even knew he was missing parts of himself. She watched him pant through his open mouth. She could see flashes of his mangled tongue flopping around like meat he was chewing. The sight made her stomach turn.

She removed the needle and thread from her pocket.

She didn't tell Teacher what she was doing. She didn't tell him she was never any good at sewing. She only knelt before him and brought her hand to his face.

She remembered very little from when she was a sick child, but she remembered the nurses and doctors would never tell her when they were going to prick her with their needles. The thought of being stabbed was supposedly worse than actually being stabbed. One particular time she hadn't even noticed she was being stabbed until she looked down and saw a needle sticking out of the crook of her elbow. She only started crying after she saw that.

But now Teacher couldn't even see the needle coming toward him. He had no way of knowing he was even going to be stabbed.

She grabbed him by the jaw. She was gentle when she did it, but it startled him and he flinched so hard it made her flinch. He jerked his face away, and she retracted her hand. He was trying to hide his face behind his raised arm, but he could only get so far from her. She grabbed his jaw again. The skin of his face was hard and firm with swelling. It almost didn't feel like real skin. She tensed her body against a shudder. She squeezed his jaw and brought his face out from behind his arm. The squeezing must have hurt him. He moaned through closed lips. Lips pinched like they were always pinched.

With her thumb she tried to pry them open. She found it hard to move her own fingers. They were too stiff, too nervous. And even as she clawed at his lips with her nails, they remained adamantly shut. She couldn't part them. She needed him to part them for her.

With her other hand she brought the needle to his face.

She pressed the tip of the needle against his closed mouth. She pressed hard. The swollen skin of his lips looked like it would burst against the needle if he didn't part his lips. He seemed to understand this. Before the needle could puncture him, he opened up.

He made way for her needle so he wouldn't be stabbed by it. She nearly sighed in relief again, but she caught herself this time.

The light of the TV was hard to see by now. It was green from some farming program, but it made the inside of his mouth look black, like he had a mouthful of chocolate syrup.

She would have to see more by feeling.

She released his jaw and slipped her left hand inside him along with the needle in her right hand. His mouth felt like how his head wound had felt in the dark. Hot, slippery. His tongue was now curling and flattening to avoid her. She pinched it between the fingers of her left hand. It didn't even feel like a tongue. It felt like folds of meat—alive meat, still hot with life, not at all like the cold things that came to her on a conveyor belt at the factory.

How many times had she dreamed of being inside this mouth? How many times had she stared at this mouth for hours, wanting just a glimpse inside and savoring every flash of pink, every crooked tooth she could see? Now she was sticking her hands inside that mouth. But it was so different when he knew she was looking, and when she knew he could taste her.

His warmth was suddenly too warm. It was scalding.

Already she wanted to retract her hands. She had to force herself to start suturing.

65

CUTE AGGRESSION

He flinched every time she poked him and he moaned like she was hurting him. He might have not even known it was a needle meant to sew him back together. He might have only thought it was a sharp thing meant to torture him. A pool of saliva and blood began forming at the back of his mouth, and he choked every time he tried to breathe. It made everything slippery and wet, and her needle almost slipped right from her grip. Her hands were making loud, wet noises as they worked along his tongue.

The procedure was too intimate. It was uncomfortable. She found herself rushing. Her suturing grew more rapid, more sloppy. She wasn't entirely sure what she was suturing to what at all. But she couldn't slow herself down. She was too anxious to finish.

When his tongue felt like one piece again, she figured she could be finished. But she realized then she didn't bring a blade to cut the thread.

The hunting knife must have been on the floor somewhere near, but she didn't want to touch that thing again after what it did to Teacher.

She brought her own mouth very close to his open one. She would sever the thread with her teeth if only to put an end to this intimacy.

He winced at the sudden proximity. He must have felt her body heat, her breath. He tried to move away, but she held him by the thread in his tongue. She put the thread in her own mouth and leaned in. His breath entered her mouth and it tasted bad, like vomit. She pressed closer and felt his crooked teeth against her lips. They were slimy and just as jagged as they looked. She felt his hard, swollen lips on her nose and chin. It was almost like she was kissing him.

He might have thought she was kissing him.

In shuddering revulsion she quickly used her own teeth to bite the thread. It was severed with a snapping sound. She pulled away at once. She expelled the smell of him from her with an exhale. She wiped her mouth, but she could still taste vomit on her lips. And when she looked at him, her heart plummeted. Even with his eyes covered, the expression on his face was clear. He looked just like he had looked when the director kissed him at the teachers' party.

Her face felt as hot as his mouth.

For a moment it was silent save for the soft sound of his blood dripping on the floor. She watched him move his tongue around in his mouth as though testing it, as though he had never had a tongue before and was trying to adjust to its presence in his mouth. His lips began contorting. His Adam's apple bobbed in his throat like he was swallowing. And then some low noises came from him, filling the silence.

They were weird noises. His vocal cords sounded like they were scraping against each other. She thought he was clearing his throat or choking on something. But after each string of noises, he paused almost expectantly. It was like he was asking her a question and then waiting for a response.

Her heart plummeted.

She realized he really was asking her a question. He really was waiting for a response.

She heard no words in his noises. It suddenly occurred to her he hadn't spoken a word since he had woken up vomiting.

Had the blows to his head rendered him an idiot? Had his cut tongue made him mute?

She looked hard at his mouth, trying to decipher the noises spilling from his lips along with the blood and saliva, but she couldn't understand a word. He didn't sound like himself. He didn't even sound like a human. He sounded more like a cow.

Her silence made him louder. He was trying so hard to talk to her he was making himself gag now. His head dropped downward, and quickly she scooted backward before he could vomit on her again. His chin touched his chest, and strings of viscous dark drool hung from his mouth. They looked like strands of black hair. She watched him retch and she almost looked away. It was such an ugly sight.

She thought it must have been the concussion making him nauseous. She knew concussions could give people nausea. She had seen that on the TV. And she was familiar with the feelings of nausea too. Her stomach had been very messed up when she was a sick child. She still thought nausea was one of the worst feelings in the world. When she was nauseous, it was all she could think about.

She lifted herself onto her knees. She reached her arms up and grabbed his wrists with her hands again. She pressed her thumbs against his inner wrists. There were pressure points in the wrists that would relieve nausea, she knew. Her mother would press her wrists like this when she was sick. She tried to do the same with Teacher to get him to stop the retching, but Teacher's wrists were cut and her fingers slipped right inside him.

He cried out again, that same animalistic yelp from before, and she flinched, took her hands away, and said, "Sorry."

The word just fell out of her mouth.

She heard herself and didn't recognize it as her own voice at first. She didn't even realize she had spoken. She hadn't wanted to speak to him at all. She had been so careful to stay quiet, but the word came out of her automatically, instinctually. She could stifle every noise, but she had no control over instincts.

His head lifted. His face was level with hers now, and it was like he was looking at her again. A silence spread between them, and she knew her voice was in his ears, making its way inside his head. He was thinking about her voice.

He opened his mouth. The dark saliva flowed from his lips, and he tried to speak again. This time, the noises began to sound more like words.

She heard them dragging against the walls of his throat, but then they got stuck as though he had a stutter. She couldn't quite make them out. She leaned forward, staring hard at his lips as though to catch the words with her eyes when they finally spilled out. When they did spill out, they came out weird and misshapen. They were pronounced strangely, as though he had a foreign accent. She could barely understand them as words. She almost didn't understand him at all.

She thought she heard him say, "Bad grades."

And then she wished she hadn't understood him.

A slow, sinking feeling afflicted her. She felt like she was being dragged right down to the floor. There was another long silence.

"Pardon me?" she said softly, politely.

"Bad grades," he said again.

And the weight of the words settled on her.

She felt her body bow beneath them.

He knew who she was.

Had he recognized her voice when she said "Sorry" just now or when she called out his name last night? Or had he known her just from her hands on him? From the sight of them on his wrists before? From the feeling of them on his waist last night? Was there no one else those hands could belong to? Was she the only person in the world who would have done this to him?

She could feel her own quickening pulse throb in her temples. The blindfold on his face suddenly looked very flimsy. It was a useless thing. A guise of safety. She could avoid being seen by his eyes. She could try to avoid being heard by his ears too. But how was she to protect herself against his brain? Against his perception of her? Against his memories? Even if he had no eyes to see her with, she was already there in his head in some form. She was someone he recognized.

"Bad grades," he said again in his strangely accented voice. And every time he said it, it made her see herself through his eyes. A girl with a hammer, bent on revenge for bad grades. A girl who cried into her hands after hitting him in the head.

But she had not cried. She never cared for grades.

"This isn't about bad grades," she said. The words came out in an urgent whisper. She found she could only speak to him in whispers. The thought of her voice in his ears was always wrong, always unnatural, yet she knew if she stayed silent he would think his own thoughts about her.

Teacher was quiet for a moment. He pinched his lips together briefly, as though turning her words over in his mind, contemplating them, tasting them. When he opened his mouth again, he said, "Something wrong?" His voice was trembling and hoarse from all his crying and yelling.

"No," she said. "No, you didn't do anything wrong." Her voice was small and cracked again. She cringed as she spoke, but she felt she had no choice but to speak. And she found herself speaking the way she spoke to any teacher, any adult. Softly. Politely. The way she was supposed to speak. Things were so different now, but he was still her teacher. There was no other way for her to speak.

He said something garbled.

She said, "Pardon?"

He said again, "Hate me?"

"*No*. Of course not." Her voice just kept getting smaller.

His brow creased and he shook his head as though to say, *Why then?*

He was trying to understand. He was trying to make sense of what was happening to him. He taught history. He told war stories. He knew about torture and death, and she supposed he thought that was what she meant for him. That was not at all what she meant for him, but how was she to explain that when he was already hurt and bleeding and strung up like a prisoner of war?

She was never any good at explaining things. She thought she didn't have a big enough vocabulary to articulate her thoughts. Or maybe her thoughts were too complex to articulate. Maybe there weren't any words that could represent what she meant. Maybe they were just meant to stay thoughts.

Her silence seemed to scare him. Her noises were all he had. His lips twitched and he tried to speak again, but his words were getting less intelligible.

"Pardon me?" she kept saying.

His breathing became hard and ragged. His heart beat so fast it moved the fabric of his shirt. And then he was making himself gag again. He couldn't speak and vomit at the same time, and this time when he retched, she didn't touch his wrists.

His head dropped down again. His chin touched his chest. An endless stream of bloody saliva spilled from his lips and pooled on the floor between his legs. And then he began making a whining noise.

"Pardon me?" she kept saying, but it seemed he couldn't hear her and didn't care to be heard himself. He was only mumbling to himself like he was half awake. Then, all of a sudden, his mumbling stopped completely. He sat there, quiet and still, hanging from his wrists by the fishing line, his head down, the crown of his head staring at her. And for a moment she could only stare back at his crown.

It was like he had shut down.

"Teacher?" she said.

She nearly thought he'd died, but the drool hanging from his lips quivered incrementally with every breath he took, and he had to be alive if he was breathing.

Tentatively, she reached out to tap his leg. "Teacher?" she said again, and when she touched his leg, she found his skin was no longer rigid.

It felt as soft as before.

She heard a noise then, like the grinding of teeth. Teacher was snoring again.

He hadn't shut down, she realized. He had only fallen asleep, almost as abruptly as he had woken up.

His concussion must have been a bad one. But she was glad for it.

She hadn't been aware of how tense her body was until she felt her muscles melt at the sound of his snoring. She knew for now no more words would come from him. No more conscious thoughts were in his head. And she could touch him again without him even feeling her hands on him.

Her hand lingered there on his leg, petting him like she was petting a dog.

It had been such a long time since she had a pet.

~

"Do you see that blood on the sidewalk?" her mother said. "That drunk must be hemorrhaging finally."

She and her mother stood at the curb in front of their apartment, waiting for a *songthaew* to come and take them to the fish factory. Under her feet were the rusty streaks of blood Teacher had left last night.

She didn't say anything. She let her mother come up with her own story. She put her hands in her pockets, and her fingers touched something cold and waxy. She shuddered, having already forgotten she had put Teacher's severed finger in her pocket. It didn't even feel like a finger.

She squinted her eyes as she looked around. It was very bright, though the sun was just rising. In the distance she saw the extent of the mess she had made only a few hours earlier. It extended further than she could see. The discounted flowers scattered on the floor. The flatbed cart halfway down the road. His dried blood, smeared into the concrete. Her hammer she couldn't even look for with her mother watching. Parts of him and parts of her all up and down the street.

It felt wrong. They were like things from another dimension. Things from her mind now on display for everyone to see.

She felt like she had to pee.

The *songthaew* pulled up to take them away. She was grateful for it, even with it packed as it was with factory women. She and her mother squeezed themselves in. Everyone smelled like fish.

~

She had seen on the TV how hard it was to completely get rid of a dead body. There was always something left behind. Some pieces, some remnants. That disturbed her. Often, in those types of movies, that was the only thing that disturbed her.

At the gutting station she ripped apart the fish that came to her, but she was deep inside her own head, thinking about how she could make that finger disappear. She contemplated flushing them down the toilet, but she thought the bones would clog the pipes. She considered stripping the flesh of Teacher's finger from the bones and then flushing only the flesh down the toilet, but then she didn't know what she would do with the bones. She supposed she could crush the bones to dust, but even then they would still be flying around somewhere in the wind.

She figured if she couldn't get rid of it, she could hide it. She could tuck it under her mattress next to her blood-stained school shirt and her private sketchbook. That was the place where she tucked everything she wanted to hide. But she didn't want to hide this finger, she wanted to destroy it.

Something about its texture upset her. It was so rigid and so cold. The blood had leaked right out of it and its color was a pale gray. She couldn't believe this thing was ever alive. She couldn't believe it was ever attached to Teacher at all. She couldn't believe it *was* Teacher. It felt more like a part of the fish she was cutting.

She shuddered. She dug her knife into the side of the fish.

She didn't know how to feel about what happened last night. She felt too many things. Her giddiness mixed with her disgust, her disgust mixed with her embarrassment, her embarrassment mixed with her fear until each emotion was indistinguishable from one another. They seemed to melt into a single emotion, one she had never felt before, one she couldn't put a name to.

She supposed it was only the discomfort of adjustment. She needed to adjust to this new life, this new reality.

Nothing was the same anymore.

It would take some getting used to.

"Whatever happened to that woman?" she heard her mother ask a nearby factory woman. "The one caught in the machine?" Her mother was nosy about these kinds of things.

"They got her out alive," the factory woman said. "They took the whole machine apart to do so. But then they ended up having to take her hand off at the hospital anyway! What a waste of time!"

Another factory woman chimed in. "It's a good thing she didn't get caught in the new machine. If that happened, she'd have nothing left. She wouldn't have even been stuck."

"What new machine?" her mother said.

"The newest machine."

There were men in orange vests who were always bringing in new machines to the factory. They had brought in a special one last night, the factory woman explained. A grinder-masher, so effective one could feed a whole fish into it and the entire thing would be reduced to fine paste, bones and all. There would be no need for a gutting station anymore. The mush the machine spat out was perfect, ready for canning.

"They said even a whale could be fed into the machine and not a bone would be found in the end product," a factory woman said, and everyone cackled with laughter. They were skeptical. They decided to take a look for themselves during their lunch break. She and her mother joined them.

Each holding fish parts, the women climbed the stairs to the third floor where the machine was. She tailed behind them. She couldn't imagine what the machine would look like. Would it look like a wood-chipper? Would it look like a giant blender?

When she finally saw it, she couldn't tell what she was looking at.

The machine was huge. One had to climb onto a platform just to reach its gaping mouth. A factory woman was meant to stand on the platform and throw the fish down into the machine below where it would supposedly be turned to a perfect, smooth mush. There was a short gate at the platform's edge for safety that could be opened for cleaning or fixing.

The factory women were still curious and skeptical. They powered the machine on themselves. It roared to life. It was violently loud, but the factory was already filled with violently loud things, and so this new machine's sound merely blended in with the rest.

The women climbed the platform together and all took turns tossing fish parts into the machine's mouth. They flinched and then laughed nervously as they watched the machine tear apart the fish in mere seconds. It was so vicious in its tearing it was almost comical. The factory women remained laughing until they saw the end product squirting out the other side of the machine and filling a large pot.

"Isn't the paste too fine?" a factory woman said.

"It's unnatural," another said. "It's almost like a liquid."

"It's like soup!"

"Maybe it'll harden later."

"I don't like it," her mother decided. "It's dangerous."

"I know," a factory woman said. "It'll put us all out of our jobs."

Eventually the factory women turned the machine off and went back to their stations.

She lingered behind.

She only stayed for a moment, not long enough for her mother to notice.

She turned the machine back on. Its sound was inaudible among the other sounds of the factory. She stood at the edge of the platform.

CUTE AGGRESSION

She leaned over the gate and stared down into the shiny new machine. Then she tossed Teacher's finger into its great mouth.

She watched the paste come out the other end. It had the consistency of porridge and was pink like salmon. It simply melted into the pot, indistinguishable from the fish mush.

~

They returned to the apartment in the early evening after work was over. Her mother went straight to the bathroom to take a shower. She would usually do the same, to wash off the fish remnants and the day's humidity and the sweat still stuck on her skin. But today, this physical discomfort from her body and her skin was second to a discomfort coming from inside her.

The apartment was very quiet. It was almost like Teacher wasn't there at all.

While her mother showered, she slipped out of the apartment and hurried up the stairs to the attic. She moved as fast as she could, but her whole body felt bruised. Throughout the day, her muscles felt like they were shrinking. Now they felt so small and tight she could barely move. Gravity felt heavier on her, too, and even as the attic's smell enveloped her, she couldn't reach up to cover her own nose. Her arms were too sore.

She walked right into the bedroom. She was stumbling over her own feet. She was anxious to see Teacher and confirm he was still here, that she hadn't simply imagined the entire acquisition of him. When she entered through the open bedroom door, she squinted through the TV light. It was dim and blue, making the room look cold, but it was stiflingly hot. It was like walking into an oven. Her eyes adjusted to the dimness, and she could make out Teacher's shape.

He was as she left him. She hadn't imagined it.

He still hung from the ceiling by his wrists, still sat on folded legs like a child. His head was still down, his chin still tucked into his chest. His torn and dirtied white shirt still hung from his body like dead skin, still quivered with each shallow breath he took.

She couldn't see his face, only the crown of his head, but he looked to be limp with sleep. She walked toward him, thinking he wouldn't hear the floorboards creak under her feet if he was asleep. But when the first floorboard creaked, it was like pressing a power button, and Teacher lifted his head up immediately.

She froze where she stood.

It seemed he wasn't asleep at all. It seemed he was only waiting.

But it wasn't his sudden movement that had startled her into a state of paralysis. It was the sight of his bare face. The sight of the blindfold around his neck like a collar.

He had shaken his blindfold off.

He was looking right at her now. And for a moment, she could only stop and look back at him.

He barely even looked like himself. His face was swollen like a fighter's, yet he trembled like a fighter would never tremble. He trembled like a dog, scared and maimed and chained. Blood and bruises discolored the skin of his face. His eyes had bruised and the swelling around them had worsened to an incredible degree, making his eyes look like huge, black mounds. She couldn't even see the whites of his eyes or his irises. She only knew he was looking at her, that his eyes were set on hers and they were unblinking.

When she could move again, she ran at him.

He shrank away from her, but his eyes were still glued to her like he was afraid to look away, like he needed to see what she would do to him next. Her hand reached out to him, and he made a noise like she had made to strike him. But she only grabbed the fabric around his neck and lifted it to his eyes again. His face was so swollen, it almost didn't fit anymore. She had to squeeze it onto him, and he cringed and groaned in apparent pain or discomfort. Once his eyes were covered again, she stumbled away from him.

She became aware of how hard she was breathing when she suddenly heard herself. It was an ugly, ragged sound, almost like an animal. She felt her face burn. She swallowed her next breath. She almost choked.

The blindfold was so tight on his swollen face she could see the outline of his eyes under it. They bulged through the fabric. In the TV light, it didn't look like he had a blindfold on at all. It looked like he had white eyes, a white face.

She shuddered.

She knew it was pointless to blind him. He already saw her. He already recognized her. He already remembered who she was, and there was no way to make him forget her. Yet she still couldn't bring herself to be seen by him, and she was scared to see him too.

He didn't look like himself right now. She couldn't tell what disturbed her more, him looking at her or him looking so different.

It was silent except for the sound of Teacher's breathing. Her eyes latched onto a stream of mucus dripping from his nose. She watched it trickle down his philtrum, then onto his pinched lips. His lips were so bloated with swelling they had perhaps doubled in size, yet he was still pinching them shut, still trying to hide his mouth, his teeth. Habits were hard to break, she figured. But she was glad for it. Otherwise she might not have been able to recognize those swollen lips as his lips.

Suddenly those lips began to twitch, and then part.

He was trying to speak again. She felt dread flourish in her stomach.

The quiet room amplified the sounds he made. It sounded like his mouth was in her ear. She heard all the wet noises of his mouth as he worked to enunciate. He worked hard. He wanted to be understood. He contorted his mouth, exaggerated the shapes of the words. She could see the black thread in his tongue like hair. Then, she could see the words he was trying to say.

"Let go, please."

He somehow sounded worse than last night. The strange accent had gotten thicker despite his effort to enunciate. She found herself cringing at the sound of him. Her brow creased. Her own lips pinched together.

Her silence prompted him to say it again. He perhaps thought she hadn't heard or understood him.

It sounded even worse the second time.

She said, "I can't let you go," just to keep him from saying it a third time. Her voice was soft and cracked, yet quick and urgent. She knew she should speak slower. She knew she should think before speaking so she wouldn't say something she would regret and so she could find the right words to express what she meant. But the words just spewed from her lips like vomit.

When her voice filled his ears, he was quiet for a moment. She knew he was turning her words over in his head again. Tasting them again.

"Hurt," he said next.

"I know," she said. "But I can't let you go."

"Hurt bad."

She looked at his gaping forehead, his bruised face, his bleeding wrists. The fishing line had cut him deep. She could barely even see the line anymore. It was buried in his skin. She watched blood drip from his wrists like she had watched the mucus drip from his nose.

They looked like streaks of thin red tendrils creeping up his arms.

She said, "It'll hurt less if you stop pulling on the line."

He pinched his lips again. Somehow, they looked different this time.

"Bag," he said then.

"Pardon me?"

"Bag."

She looked at the open bedroom door. From where she stood she could see his bag on the living room floor where she had left it.

"I have your bag," she mumbled.

He exhaled, almost like a sigh of relief, and he nodded his head. "Bag," he said.

"Do you want something in your bag?" she said.

He nodded his head again so fervently it looked like a convulsion.

She left the room to retrieve the bag. She bent down to grab it, and her sore muscles exploded with pain. She almost made a noise. The bag was very heavy. The weight of it nearly dragged her right to the ground as she picked it up. She had to hold it in her arms like a baby as she brought it back to him.

His head followed her as she walked toward him, like he was tracking her by the sound of her footsteps.

"What is it you want, Teacher?" she said.

He said something garbled.

"Pardon me?"

"Wallet," he said.

She opened the bag. She looked through his belongings.

It was almost as intimate as putting her hands inside his mouth.

She was just as uncomfortable.

She had never touched his belongings before. There was always a distance between her and him, a buffer separating them. Now her hands touched many of his things.

The bag was cluttered like a boy's bag, things thrown in carelessly and fished for later. She took things out so she could find the wallet easier. She removed history books first. They were heavy and their pages were tattered from use. She dropped them on the floor, too sore to set them down carefully. They made the whole room shake as they landed. It seemed to startle Teacher. He made a choked noise.

Next she found many little cassette tapes, all containing songs he liked to listen to in his classroom. She knew they were all old country songs. She knew all the songs he liked to listen to.

She let them fall to the floor.

Her hand came in contact with something small and cold then. She grabbed it and removed it. It was a small tube. She squinted at it. She couldn't tell what it was. She opened the cap and found a stick of skin-colored makeup.

She frowned.

Why would he have this in his bag?

Did he wear makeup regularly? She didn't think so. He sweated too much to wear makeup, and his skin had visible blemishes.

She thought of the day after the hammer incident, how smooth his forehead had looked. She thought of him in the bathroom, examining his forehead in the mirror.

She stared at the tube of makeup in her hand. Had Teacher worn makeup to cover the wound she had made on him?

Her frown deepened. She quickly turned her hand over and let the tube drop to the floor. The noise it made as it hit the floor made it seem like she had thrown it.

She shoved her hands back inside the bag, searching impatiently now for the wallet he wanted. She felt something bubbling in her chest. The familiar tendrils of growing frustration.

Her hand touched something thin and glossy. It felt like another book. She feared it was the yearbook. Her hand clawed at it as she pulled it out. She looked at it, expecting to see the white yearbook cover. But instead she found a cover with a familiar hand-drawn chicken on it.

It was a children's book of the Thai alphabet, the same one she had used to learn to read, the same one her mother used too. It was for children, though, or for foreigners who didn't yet know how to read.

Why would Teacher have such a book?

He already knew how to read. There was no reason for him to have such a book for himself.

Did he have a child?

She frowned so hard a shudder ran through her. She had never considered it a possibility for him to have a child. She didn't like the idea. It was so foreign, so hard to imagine, so different from who she thought he was.

She threw the book on the floor, only wanting to get it away from her like it was something gross or dangerous. But the sound it made slapping the floor was an angry sound. It made Teacher flinch, and then tremble. He must have thought she was angry.

The next time she stuck her hand in his bag, she finally found his wallet.

It must have been a nice leather wallet once, but now it was old and gray and sticky. She unfolded it and looked inside. The first thing she saw was a condom. She frowned again. It looked more like a scowl. She felt the urge to throw the wallet like she had thrown the alphabet book. She had to swallow the urge.

She breathed sharply and looked through the rest of the wallet. There were wads of money, a couple thousand baht. There were credit cards.

There was a photograph.

She removed the photograph. It was small, with jagged edges, evidently cut out of a bigger picture. It was of a woman. Older than Teacher or younger, she couldn't tell. Pretty or ugly, she couldn't tell, either. She only saw a woman squinting as she smiled at her, making one eye look bigger than the other. And the sight seemed to amplify the feeling of frustration swirling in her chest. It felt like her chest was filling like a balloon. It felt like it would burst.

It felt like she was in that math class again.

"What about your wallet?" she said. Her tongue was sharp, but her voice trembled.

"Money," he said.

"What about your money?"

"Yours."

Her brow creased. "I don't want your money," she mumbled.

He said a long string of unintelligible words then.

"What?" she said.

He repeated himself slowly. It sounded something like, "What do you want, then?"

He still didn't understand. She still didn't know how to explain. But the longer she remained silent, the more time he had to think things about her. He was already thinking things about her. He had thought she was upset about bad grades. Then he thought she could be bribed with money.

She felt the need to say something, or else her silence would be another answer to him.

The words tumbled out of her mouth awkwardly and desperately.

"I just want to look at you."

And then a silence spread over them.

CUTE AGGRESSION

It was the same kind of silence that fell over that math class when she had peed herself.

She knew it was a mistake as soon as she said it. It was a mistake to ever speak to him at all.

He had wanted to understand. But she realized she didn't want him to understand. And now she couldn't speak. There were no words in her head to be spoken. Her mind became terribly numb. It was like she didn't even have a mind. And the sudden absence of a mind made her feel like she was nothing but a body.

Teacher couldn't seem to speak either. Even with parts of him covered, he looked the most frightened he had ever been.

She felt the embarrassment burning her skin like fire.

She looked at the wallet still in her hands. It was a compulsion to distract herself, to take her mind off herself by redirecting her focus. Her fingers began to sweat as they wedged themselves into the wallet's folds and crevices. She pulled out a card. It was an identification card. She looked at it, and at once her insides felt like they were melting. They felt like they would fall right out of her.

His ID photo was a good photo, too cheap and rushed to be edited. It looked like how he would look in her head. That sense of affection arose in her, mixing with the frustration. But she couldn't tell if it was diluting the frustration or intensifying it.

She looked up from the photo. She looked at Teacher strung up before her.

He was the one she always looked to in order to get away from herself, to shift her focus away from herself. But now, as she looked at him, she could only see the marks she left on him. She looked at his swollen face bulging out around the blindfold, at the fluids dripping off him, at his features twitching with fear or anticipation.

There was barely any resemblance to his ID photo.

She dropped the card on the floor. She dropped the wallet on the floor too. And then she dumped the bag onto the floor. It made a loud sound. She could see Teacher flinch again out of the corner of her eye as she stormed out of the bedroom.

She felt a fire in her like the one burning her skin. But it wasn't embarrassment, it was a sense of urgency just like the one she felt last night, the one that sent her scooting down the stairs on her bottom and crawling to her apartment on all fours in search of a needle and thread to put him back together with.

In a frenzy she searched the old lady's apartment. She knew she would find nothing but fishing supplies in the bedroom closet. There was nothing she could use in there. She went to search the bathroom instead.

It smelled equally of good and bad things. Bodily waste mixed with fragrant soaps. There was a humming sound in here, almost like a machine. She soon figured it was the sound of water flowing down through the rusty pipes for her mother's shower downstairs. A vague thought floated through her racing mind. She wondered if the old lady had heard her life just as she had heard the old lady's life.

She shook the thought and the discomfort that came with it from her mind as soon as it flitted inside. Her hands darted out and grabbed anything she could use. A worn toothbrush, a folded tube of tooth-paste, a used bar of soap, a brush with gray hair still wedged in its bristles. Her hands were full, but she still felt she needed more. This couldn't possibly be enough to bring Teacher back to who he was.

She left the bathroom and went to the kitchenette. On her way there she felt something rough and scratchy under her bare feet. She realized too late she had stepped right on top of the old lady's corpse stain.

It felt like short, coarse hair from some animal, and it was warm with the rising heat from outside. It almost felt like it was alive.

She hurried off it. She rubbed the soles of her feet on the legs of her pants as though to rub away the feeling. But she couldn't seem to rid herself of the feeling no matter how much she rubbed.

Her skin crawled and bubbled with goosebumps as though to shake off the feeling.

In the kitchenette she went straight for the freezer. She found packs of frozen meat wrapped in thin plastic. She grabbed one. She didn't know what kind of meat it was. It was dark and oddly shaped. It was so cold it had ice on it. It burned her hand and stuck to her skin no matter how she gripped it. She figured it must have been fro-zen for a long time.

She searched the cabinets then. She found seasonings and bleach and drain cleaner. Under the sink, however, she found a roll of duct tape. Her heart surged in her chest. She nearly gasped. She reached for it so fast the bar of soap slipped out of her hand. She didn't bother to pick it up again. She was so relieved to find the tape.

With her arms full, she leapt over the stain on the carpet and ran back to the bedroom.

She dropped everything on the floor except the duct tape. They thudded noisily and their weight made the floorboards creak. Teacher tensed and flinched like he did with every noise and every vibration. His head jerked in the direction of the commotion. She was being so loud, but she couldn't help herself.

She fumbled with the roll of tape. When she unrolled it, it made a painfully loud noise. It was an assault on the ears. It made both of them wince.

Quickly, she went to him and wrapped duct tape over his eyes, right over the blindfold. The feeling of it seemed to scare him even more than the sound of it. He made noises like he was pleading with her. She could just barely make out the pleading words. She didn't want to make them out. She tried to tune out the sound. She said nothing. She didn't want to speak to him ever again. She just wanted to look at him.

She kept wrapping the duct tape around his head, over his eyes, wrapping it too many times like she had wrapped his wrists with the fishing line. Her hands were wet with her sweat and his fluids, and she struggled to rip the tape. She used her teeth to cut it, and when she brought her face close to him, the smell of him invaded her. He smelled even more sour than before. He smelled like he was food going bad.

When she was finished, she dropped the roll of tape onto the floor with the rest of the supplies. She looked at his duct taped face and felt a bit better. He wouldn't be able to shake the duct tape off. It gave her a sense of security, like locking a door. But his face was shiny with all sorts of fluids reflecting the TV light. Blood from his wounds, snot running from his nose, tears from his face, sweat all over him. His forehead wound leaked not just blood but a clear fluid like water. It made his whole face very wet, and she feared it would make the adhesive unstick, and the duct tape would come right off.

She looked around the room for something to dry him with. Her eyes went to his shirt.

The shirt was filthy, and it looked bizarre, torn as it was. The front of it was covered in all sorts of fluids and colors. And, admittedly, she thought he looked weird with a torn shirt and nothing else on.

She reached out, grabbed the collar of the shirt, and began tearing it like she had done last night. But she didn't stop after tearing off a single strip.

When Teacher realized what she was doing, he began to cry.

It surprised her. She paused her tearing and looked at him again.

At first she thought she was somehow hurting him. But soon she started to think he just didn't want to be naked.

She continued tearing.

She ripped the fabric in many places. It cleaved along the seams almost like meat. He cried the whole time, but it was a different type of cry. He had his head down and he sobbed through his nose with his mouth closed. It was quiet, suppressed. Almost like his laugh. It sounded more like a human this time. It sounded more like him.

She peeled the shirt off him in pieces until he was naked. He kept his head down like he was ashamed, like if he couldn't hide his body, he would hide his face. He didn't want to be looked at like this.

Strangely, she didn't want to look at him either.

She had drawn him naked, imagined him naked, but she had never before seen him completely naked with her own eyes. And although the opportunity was now before her, her eyes were flickering too restlessly to look at him. She couldn't bring herself to look. It was different when he knew she was looking.

She almost wanted to put the shirt back on him, but it was already torn into so many pieces. She wouldn't have even known where to begin with piecing it back together.

She balled the pieces of his shirt in her hands. She knelt before him, nearly mirroring his position. She wiped the blood and fluid from his face with the ball of fabric. She wanted to get him as dry as possible so it wouldn't dilute the adhesive of the tape. But as she wiped, the fluids just kept pouring, mixing together until she didn't even know what kind of fluid she was sopping up.

She felt the frustration quiver in her. She stopped wiping him. She tossed the ball of fabric aside, and already, he was wet again.

His forehead wound just kept weeping.

She supposed it would take some time to close and heal.

The wound was trying to scab over. Some strands of his hair were stuck in the forming scabs. She reached out and carefully pulled the strands loose. Then she slicked his hair off his forehead completely to let the wound breathe. His hair felt oily with blood and other fluids. She grabbed the brush on the floor and combed his hair straight back. He wore it like this sometimes to school. She hoped it would make him look more like himself. But there was so much blood in his hair, it changed its color and texture. And his hair swept back like this looked more like curtains pulled apart, putting his face on full display.

A pit tightened in her stomach.

He looked worse like this. She could see his features more clearly, and his features were lumpy with swelling. He looked like a different person. She reminded herself it was just the swelling making him look different. He was still her teacher under it all. Swelling was temporary. Bruises were too. His body was already trying to heal itself. Soon his wounds would close. The swelling would go down and away. The bruises would fade. He would look more like himself eventually.

She wanted to quicken the process.

She picked up the pack of frozen meat from the floor. She knelt before him, practically mirroring his position. Carefully, she reached out and held the frozen meat to the side of his face like an ice pack. After the initial shock of the cold, Teacher grew still and quiet. He seemed confused again.

For a long time it was silent save for Teacher's hitching breath. And then she felt a heavy kind of awkwardness creep in. A kind of awkwardness that crushes and suffocates.

She bit down on her tongue against it. She hated awkwardness. Her eyes darted about, trying to find something to focus on, to get away from herself and the feeling afflicting her. Her eyes latched onto the mucus trickling from his nose onto his lip again.

It was like he knew she was staring at his mouth. His lips immediately parted. He started to speak again.

"Let down," he said.

She bit her tongue harder. She didn't want to respond. But it would be even more awkward if she didn't.

She said, "I can't let you go. I told you already."

"Let *down*."

She paused. He wasn't asking to be let go. He was asking to be let down. The fishing line must have been hurting him. This position must have been uncomfortable.

She looked at the duct tape around his face, wrinkled and thickly layered. The thought hadn't even crossed her mind before, but she now realized she could use the duct tape to bind him too. She looked at his bloody, torn wrists, at the fishing line buried in his skin. Duct tape wouldn't cut his skin the way the fishing line did. It would be a good replacement.

She was about to remove the meat from his face and retrieve the roll of tape, but she stopped herself short.

If she let him down, even for a moment, would he not overpower her?

She looked at his body. She couldn't think of any ways to confine him with the tape that would secure him as well as the fishing line did. The line hurt him, but it kept him from hurting her.

Would Teacher hurt her?

She couldn't imagine him hurting her. She realized there were many ways she couldn't imagine him, but that didn't mean they weren't possible.

"I'll think about it," she said softly.

There was a pause, and then he said, "Please."

His voice nearly sounded like her own now, so small and cracked, like he was afraid or embarrassed of being heard.

She cringed. It was like listening to herself.

"I said I'll think about it," she said, pressing the meat to his swollen mouth so he wouldn't speak anymore.

Every time he spoke, a smell was propelled out of his mouth, a foul smell. It smelled like stale vomit and blood.

They sat there in silence for a while. She held the meat to his face until her hand was burning and constricting from the cold. When she couldn't stand it anymore, she tried to take the meat away from his face, but it was so cold it stuck to his skin. He cried out in pain, and she hissed out an apology on instinct. She peeled the meat off him carefully so he wouldn't cry out. Then she had to peel the meat off her own hand. It was stuck to her skin too.

She shook it off her hand impatiently, flinging it onto the floor. Teacher's face was red where the meat had touched but no less swollen. The skin of her hand was just as red. She rubbed her hand on her pants, trying to rub the redness away.

She reached for the toothbrush on the floor. The smell of his breath still lingered in the air. She didn't know if it was actually lingering or if her mind just remembered the smell.

She squeezed a glob of toothpaste onto the bristles. Then she grabbed his jaw again, just like when she sutured his tongue.

He was less resistant now. Perhaps he knew she was only trying to help him. The skin under his chin felt prickly, like sandpaper. The feeling surprised her. She thought something else might have gone wrong, that he had developed a rash or something. But upon examination, she found little hairs sprouting on the skin of his face. They were like little black needles in his skin, and she felt an urge to pluck them out of him. She had never seen hair on Teacher's face before. She didn't even think him capable of growing facial hair. The thought never crossed her mind. His skin was always clean and smooth.

She bit down on her tongue and inserted the toothbrush into his mouth.

She started to brush his teeth. Immediately, his face contorted and made a long, drawn out noise, like he was in pain. He squirmed and twisted and wouldn't keep still. She gripped his jaw with her hand to steady him and keep his head lifted.

His tongue was in terrible condition. Perhaps that was why he was cringing. She avoided his tongue as best she could, but it was hard to avoid when it was enlarged with swelling. It looked misshaped, too. It seemed she had stitched it on twisted.

She brushed his teeth hard. His cries began to evolve. It sounded like he was trying to say something now. His mangled tongue darted around in his mouth. It was even harder to avoid like this. She tightened her grip. She brushed his teeth harder.

The toothpaste turned red. His gums bled.

And then, his teeth fell out as she brushed them.

Just like when his tongue had been half severed, it took a moment to understand what was happening.

The teeth loosened in their sockets and scattered onto the floor.

They sounded like little pebbles hitting the ground.

When she finally realized what happened, she hurried to pick them up. They were slippery and kept falling out of her hands. They made so much noise. She put them in her pocket, and all the while Teacher had gone silent.

His noises had stopped completely. He only sat there, still like a corpse and bleeding from the mouth. It seemed he was too shocked to do anything but sit and bleed.

He must have heard his teeth hit the floor. He must have felt them come out of his gums, too.

~

The sun was setting. She didn't have much time before her mother noticed her absence like a teacher. She hurried down the street, nearly tripping over the cracks in the sidewalk. She wasn't paying attention to where she was walking. She was lost in her head, thinking she had always loved his teeth.

They were stained and crooked, the bottom ones more so than the top ones, but she thought they were cute. More than anything, she loved how he sought to hide them, how he pinched his lips together into a frown whenever he wanted to laugh or smile. She thought that was cute too.

How could they have just fallen out like that?

They simply loosened and fell out like dead hair coming off on the brush. But teeth didn't grow back like hair.

Had she hit him in the head so hard it knocked his teeth loose?

She felt her stomach turn.

She had only wanted him unconscious so she could take him and then have him. That was all the hammer was meant for. But now parts of him were changing. Parts of him were falling right off him. And now she could barely understand why she had even wanted him at all.

Why had she wanted him in the first place?

She supposed she only wanted to have him.

Why did she want to have him?

Why did anyone want to have anything?

She figured people are their possessions. They are what they own.

She followed the trails of blood down the sidewalk. She dragged her feet over them, trying to rub them out of the concrete, but it seemed they had already stained the ground. There was no rubbing them out. They would stay there as long as they wanted to stay there. The attempt to get rid of them only hurt her sore legs even more.

She soon found what she had come for. Meters from the front of the tropical fish shop, she saw her hammer on the ground. No one had moved it. She doubted anyone had even seen it. Rarely anyone walked this road. Now that the school term was over, probably no one walked it at all.

The hammer was coated in blood like paint. She picked it up. It was like picking up an old part of herself. Belongings were strange like that, she thought.

She began to walk back to the apartment. She was sweaty and sticky. She was getting slower. Her feet were scraping, making noises against the concrete. Her body was too tired to rush anymore. She found she couldn't control the way she moved. She couldn't force herself to quicken her step. She realized it was fatigue slowing her down. She hadn't slept since that time in her vent at school, right before the teachers' party. That felt so long ago. It made this whole ordeal feel like one never-ending day.

As she struggled to walk, a *soi* dog emerged, dirty and bulbous and stray. Its fur looked rough. She couldn't tell what its natural color was, but it looked a bit brown, a bit yellow. It smiled at her the way dogs smile. It followed her, looking up at her. She stopped and it stopped with her. It lapped its tongue like it was hungry. She stood there, looking down at it. She clutched her blood-stained hammer in her hand.

The dog had no idea such a thing could hurt it. Just a few strikes could change it forever. It had no idea she could bring it down on its head so easily. The only thing she needed was a will to do so.

She had no will to do so.

Oblivious, the dog just kept looking up at her like it wanted something from her.

She held her hammer out to it, thinking it was attracted to the scent of Teacher's blood. But the dog only sniffed the metal a few times before looking up at her again. It didn't seem interested in the blood or the hammer.

It began to venture closer to her, digging its nose against her legs now. She thought it was sniffing her crotch at first, but then she realized it was only sniffing her pocket.

She reached into the pocket and pulled out a fistful of Teacher's teeth.

Nearly half his bottom teeth had come out while she brushed them. There were five teeth in total, all molars on the right side of his mouth. The dog began to sniff at her palm. She let it sniff the teeth. But then, suddenly, the dog's tongue darted out.

It began lapping up the teeth.

"No!" she cried. It was loud enough to make the dog startle and turn away. She turned her hand into a fist and tried to snatch the teeth away from the dog's mouth, but it only made the teeth go flying in the air. They scattered all over the place. The dog began running away, jiggling and lapping its tongue like it was eating something.

She got down on her knees and picked the teeth from the ground but only found four. She looked around frantically for the fifth, but it was nowhere to be found.

She figured the dog had eaten it.

She whipped her head up and searched for the dog. It was already far down the *soi*, but it was running slowly, almost leisurely, like she wasn't a terrible threat to it. She rose from the ground. She started after it. She wanted to chase it and get the tooth from it. But then she figured the tooth was already in its stomach, and she stopped in her tracks.

She didn't want to dig it out.

Her throat grew tight and started to hurt. She felt like she would cry.

"Dumb dog," she muttered. Bones weren't edible. Even dogs should know that.

But then she thought of the shiny new machine at the fish factory. She thought of all the fish bones somehow being turned into edible mush.

She looked at the four teeth in her hands. She stroked them like she had once stroked his blood dried into her school shirt. The saliva on them had gone dry by now, giving the teeth an almost matte finish. It was strange. Teeth weren't meant to be dry. It was like they weren't even teeth anymore. They didn't feel like teeth, but they still looked like teeth. They looked like *his* teeth.

She saw the familiar stains on them. She saw the jagged edges. She saw that some of them looked like fangs.

His face had changed so much, but his teeth remained the same.

She closed her hand around the teeth. Their jagged edges dug into her palm, like a little bite.

She couldn't help but think these teeth were the only parts of him she would have left if he kept falling apart like he was.

She picked out one of Teacher's teeth. She went for a particularly jagged one. She thought she recognized this one. She thought it was close to the front of his mouth, jammed next to his canine. Then she thought of the dog lapping up his tooth.

Timidly, as though embarrassed, she snuck it into her own mouth.

She held it with her tongue. She pushed it flat against the roof of her mouth. She turned it over a few times. The saliva in her mouth began to pool. She swallowed around the tooth. And it was like her mouth was his mouth. Her saliva wetted the tooth, making it feel like it was supposed to. Her tongue felt what Teacher's tongue must have felt. Her tongue tasted what he must have tasted. It tasted like many things, too many to distinguish.

She felt like she was with him without actually being with him. It was like stroking his blood on her school shirt so long ago. Somehow, it was better than actually being with him in that attic.

She continued to suck on it like a piece of hard candy.

~

The body wasn't meant to be in reality for so long. It couldn't withstand it. She felt her own body beginning to break down, to deteriorate. She needed to get some sleep.

CUTE AGGRESSION

Her head felt pounds heavier. The space behind her eyes was filled with an immense, crushing pressure. Yet as she lay down in her bed, she couldn't get comfortable enough to sleep. Her body was too sore to ignore, and she felt imprisoned by it. She couldn't drift away from her body when it was all she could feel, all she could think about. When she pulled the covers over her head she could smell herself too. She remembered she still hadn't showered.

Through the blankets, she could hear Teacher above her making the floorboards creak. The bedroom he was in was directly above hers. She could almost feel the weight of him on her.

Suddenly she could hear more than just creaks.

Another sound bled through the floorboards and dripped right onto her. She didn't know what she was hearing at first, only that it reverberated through the floor and walls. It nearly sounded like it was coming from the walls again, like the building itself was crying.

She flung the blankets from her head, and then it sounded like there was an animal in the attic. But she knew it must have been Teacher making those noises in his throat. Noises just like an animal. He was quickly getting louder and more frantic. He was crying out, she realized. Crying out like he was in trouble. Like something had gone wrong. Like he was being attacked.

Soon he was thumping against the floorboards. He made the whole apartment shake. It was like he was grinding his knees into the floor. It was like he would break right through the floor, come right down on her.

She struggled to get out of bed. She didn't know how to move her body when it was sore like this. It was almost like it wasn't her body anymore.

She grabbed her hammer, thinking she would need it if Teacher was being attacked.

She ventured out of her bedroom and found the living room looked just like Teacher's room, lit only with TV light.

Her mother was asleep on the couch in front of her *lakorn* again. It was the same every night. She couldn't tell one night from the next. Even the *lakorn* on the screen looked the same every night.

She walked past her mother. She slipped out of the apartment. She hurried up the stairs. She entered the attic, and then Teacher's cries were all she could hear. He sounded so hoarse. It must have hurt to cry out like that. But even when his vocal cords sounded like they were ripping and tearing, he kept crying just as hard.

She entered the bedroom.

In the flashing TV light, she could barely see what was attacking him, but she heard their buzzing.

Swarming around the bloody stump where his finger used to be were fattened corpse flies, leftover from when the old lady died.

Teacher writhed against his binds. He struggled to shake the flies off, but the fishing line held him in place. His disfigured hand could only twitch each time one of them brushed against him. They were fat and aggressive and loud enough to hear even amid Teacher's cries. They must have gorged themselves on the old lady's corpse. Now they wanted to gorge themselves on Teacher. They must have thought he was dead.

She went to him with her hands outstretched to swat the flies. He must have heard her approach, for he shrank away from her like she was a corpse fly. She swatted the flies away, waving her hand around them almost lazily. Very quickly they dispersed.

They were just flies, after all.

She stifled a sigh. She dropped her hammer on the floor. It made a loud sound. It made Teacher wince and choke.

He must have no longer felt the flies on him or heard their buzzing. He slowly began to calm down. He stopped his crying but was left hiccupping and gasping and drooling. His drool was thick and black with blood. His hand, the one the flies had been eating, was shaking badly. The stump where his index finger used to be squirted blood with every twitch despite the tourniquet she had made for it. His wrists squirted blood too. He had cut himself to the bone in his attempt to get away from the flies. She couldn't even see the fishing line anymore, it was so deep in his wrists.

"They were just flies, Teacher," she said.

But Teacher still trembled so hard he made the floorboards creak. It would sound as loud as bombs below him. She would never be able to sleep with that noise.

"Could you be a little quieter, please, I can't sleep," she said, her voice as soft and polite as before. She conformed to the roles she was expected to play. The expected etiquette of conversation. She was talking to her teacher, after all. Even if he was strung up and looking so different, he was still her teacher.

There was a pause. Still sniveling, he said, "Sorry." He sounded more like a child than her teacher. A child who was just learning how to speak, at that.

She frowned. When he didn't sound like her teacher she didn't know how to talk to him. He sounded like a child. Did that mean she should talk to him like one? The formalities seemed displaced, yet she still stuck to them.

"It's okay," she said, perhaps too politely. "Can you just quiet down, please?"

"Okay," he said. "But hurt."

She was silent for a moment. She looked at the duct tape over his eyes. The edges of the duct tape were peeling, like he had tried to take it off himself. His blood and other fluids pooled in the crevices of the peeled edges.

She said, "Is there anything I can do to make you more comfortable?"

"Let down, please."

"I can't let you down," she said. "I told you that already."

He sniffed, said, "Okay."

"Is there anything else I could do, Teacher?"

His lips pinched. Swollen as they were, they looked like they would burst. When they parted again, he said, "TV."

She didn't understand him at first.

"Pardon me?"

"TV," he said again.

She looked at the TV. Advertisements were now playing, painfully overwhelming, manic and bright as though to traumatize them into the brain. She supposed that was what advertisements aimed to do. Dig themselves in so as to not be forgotten. The only way to not be forgotten was to traumatize.

"What about the TV?" she said.

"Watch TV," he said.

She thought of her mother sleeping on the couch downstairs in the light of the *lakorn*. Would the TV help Teacher sleep just like it helped her mother sleep? She supposed the TV was a way to escape reality, just like sleep. Perhaps that's why people often used TV to put themselves to sleep.

She went over to the TV. The floor groaned under every step like she was hurting it. She couldn't crouch down with her muscles sore like this. She struggled to reach for the controls on the TV's side. She unmuted the TV but kept the volume low.

"Better?" she said.

"Watch TV," he said.

"Yes, you can watch TV."

"Watch," he said. "Watch TV."

"Watch . . ."

She realized he wanted to watch with his own eyes. He wanted her to take the duct tape off his face.

She shook her head and realized too late he couldn't see her. She was forced to speak. "You can listen to it," she said. "It's the same thing."

She knew it wasn't the same thing. He seemed to know that too. He pinched his lips even tighter. They really looked like they would burst.

"What channel would you like?" she said uneasily.

"News," he said.

She pressed the buttons on the TV, flipped through the channels until she reached a news station. She saw the news anchors, a man and a woman, seated at their desk. She stared at the news program, and it suddenly struck her Teacher might one day be on the news. She supposed that's why he wanted to watch it. To see if anyone had noticed his disappearance, if anyone would ever know what happened to him.

A shudder ran through her.

She didn't want people to know about what happened. She didn't want any trouble.

She reached down and changed the channel again. The TV turned black as it changed. The news disappeared, and when the light reappeared, it was a *lakorn* on the screen. The same one her mother had just fallen asleep to.

The room was filled with its soft blue light, its soft music.

Teacher said nothing, but his silence was like words.

She stood there for a moment, watching the *lakorn*, the one Teacher was listening to, the one her mother had fallen asleep to. And she knew that no matter who was watching, they were watching through the same eyes.

She didn't watch TV much anymore. She had gotten sick of seeing herself all the time. A girl on the TV was every girl. It didn't matter how she looked, how she acted, what role she played. All that mattered was only how she was perceived. And how she was perceived was how every girl was perceived.

She had watched enough TV to know what people were thinking when they looked at her. She found she couldn't talk to people without knowing what they were thinking. She couldn't form a relationship without discomfort because perception, she thought, was degradation. If not literal, then assumed. When people looked at her, they imagined her in a role.

It was a realization that caused her to go further inside herself. She liked it better in her head anyway. She liked it better seeing through her own eyes rather than the TV's eyes. She preferred seeing things other than herself. She liked it when she was looking without being looked at.

If the TV taught her anything, it taught her she was meant to be looked at.

A woman was meant to be looked at. She was meant to be attractive. To be desired. To be nice to look at.

Did her eyes mean anything? What were eyes for? Would it matter if a woman had no eyes at all? Would it make any difference?

It made a difference to her. She'd like to keep her eyes. She'd want nothing else.

She could hear Teacher's wet breathing over the *lakorn*. She didn't know which sound was worse.

She went to the TV and muted it again. One terrible sound was more tolerable than two, she thought, but when the TV's sound disappeared, it seemed to amplify not only the sound of Teacher's breathing, but her own breathing as well.

Her breathing was ragged. She hadn't even realized how hard she had been breathing. She knew he must have heard her just as she heard herself.

She brought her hands to her mouth so hard and so fast she slapped herself.

She muffled her sounds. She swallowed her breaths, inhaled and exhaled as slowly as possible until she could no longer hear herself and he could no longer hear her.

The only sound now remaining in the room was his breathing.

She could slow her own breathing. She could turn off the TV, turn off its sound. But there was no way to turn him off.

Was there?

She looked at her hammer on the floor, still stained with his blood. She thought of how she bashed his head in with it, how quickly he had turned off.

She went to the hammer. She picked it up. The creaks in the floorboards showed him where she was, and his head followed her as though he could actually see her.

She stood behind him. She held the hammer up to the back of his head. He was trying to crane his neck to look behind him again, and he didn't even have eyes to see with. With her free hand she pushed his head down until his chin touched his chest. He looked very much like a man about to be executed, and her hand on his head was very much like the hand of an executioner.

She raised the hammer, and then she thought he looked more like an animal about to be slaughtered.

But she didn't mean to slaughter him. She didn't mean to execute him. She only wanted to turn him off again, like she had turned him off before. Maybe if her strike was a good one, she could knock the memories from his head and the sight from his eyes too.

She prepared to bring her hammer down. Her hand sweated like it was drooling with anticipation. But before she brought it down, she froze.

She thought, Would this not change him even more?

The hammer had made his face change so much. It had made a gaping hole in his forehead. It distorted his speech. It knocked his teeth loose.

What more would it do to him?

She pursed her lips. She clenched her teeth. She gripped the hammer so hard it hurt her hand, so hard it made her whole arm shake.

She dropped her arm.

The weight of the hammer nearly pulled her shoulder out of its socket.

Her arm and the hammer remained swinging by her side.

"Just be quiet, please," she said politely. The way she was supposed to. "I can't sleep, is all."

He didn't say anything. He didn't even lift his head again. It was like he knew she had a hammer in her hands.

~

She slept not at all. Teacher didn't seem to sleep either. She heard him crying quietly the whole night. It wasn't just his noise keeping her awake but the weight of him upstairs. She was starting to get accustomed to his sounds, like a constant buzzing in her ears. She didn't think she'd ever get accustomed to the weight of him though.

When she rose from bed, it was midday. She rose to the sound of Teacher hoarse crying and to the smell of cooking. As she crawled out of bed, she felt like nothing but parts. A hungry stomach. A heavy head. Tired ears. Sore muscles.

She found her mother squatting on the living room floor, making *kanom jeen* for lunch on an electric stove. She stirred meatballs into the yellow curry base in the pot, then she cut red and green chilis up in her own hand. All the while, Teacher's cries made the whole apartment pulse.

She sat on the couch stiffly before her mother.

"Enjoying your break?" her mother said when she saw her. "Seems like it. You slept past noon!"

She said nothing. She only watched her mother cook amid Teacher's noises. Her mother made no sign she heard anything at all. She couldn't understand it. She knew her mother was hard of hearing, but Teacher's noises were so loud one didn't even need ears to hear them. One could feel them.

She kept her eyes fixed on her mother, dreading the moment she did feel or hear something. And after an especially loud cry from Teacher, it seemed the moment came.

Her mother paused her cutting and looked up at her with a furrowed brow.

She became even more stiff. Panic surged in her painfully. She was certain her mother had heard Teacher that time. Her mind raced as she tried to conjure up ways to explain it away. But before she could even open her mouth, her mother said, "I used to make this for you when you were sick, you know. Do you remember?"

She was frozen with confusion now. She looked at the yellow *kanom jeen* her mother was making, and then the relief rushed in. It was perhaps more painful than the panic. It rendered her speechless for a moment. The sound of Teacher crying filled the silence, and her mother continued staring at her, waiting for an answer.

She managed to shake her head and say she didn't remember.

That was true. She didn't remember much from that time. She had been very young and very sick.

Her mother looked back down at her hands and resumed her cutting. "*Kanom jeen* was one of your favorites."

A bit much for a sick three-year-old, she thought, then said so.

"I fed you everything when you were sick!" her mother said, laughing. "I fed you every delicious food I could find or make! You ate better than rich people! I was certain you were going to die. And I thought if you were going to die, you should die on a full stomach. You should die eating delicious food."

She frowned, not remembering any of the food she ate when she was sick.

"But then you didn't die," her mother said. "I think the food tasted so good, you didn't want to die anymore." Her mother laughed very hard then, so hard she had to stop cutting again. "You didn't want to die, you wanted to live so you could keep on eating!"

Her mother's laughter overlapped with Teacher's cries. It nearly made it sound like Teacher was laughing too. She even found herself smiling a bit.

When her mother's laughter died down, she wiped tears from her eyes. "I think the food made you get better faster," her mother said. "It revived you in ways I never even thought possible! You had gone mute for months, and all of a sudden, after eating some, you were speaking again!"

At that, her ears perked.

"Really?" she said.

Her mother made a noise of assent, then dumped the chilis into the yellow water. "You were a bit fat for a sick girl," her mother said. "But there are worse things to be."

"I was fat?" she said.

"Fat and weird looking."

"Weird how?"

"You didn't even look like yourself. You changed so fast. I looked at you one day, and all of a sudden you looked like a different person. You looked *dead*. It was scary."

She thought of Teacher in the attic, how different he looked and how different he sounded.

Her mother fell silent for a moment. The yellow water in the pot began to bubble on the electric stove. Steam rose. Teacher no longer sounded like he was laughing. It sounded like he was weeping.

To lighten things, perhaps, her mother said, "But thankfully the food resurrected you. And now you look like yourself again. You look better than yourself! See? A sick person needs to eat."

~

Eating was like sleeping. She ate the *kanom jeen* with her mother, and she felt a little more energized. As they ate, Teacher grew quiet in the attic. It was almost like her stomach was his stomach.

After lunch she helped her mother clean up. Then her mother curled up on the couch to watch TV. She knew a nap was coming. The TV always put her mother to sleep.

As soon as her mother started snoring, she crept to the kitchen and gathered some leftovers in a bowl. She cut up the rice noodles so they could be eaten with a spoon. Then she filled a glass with water from the tap.

With the bowl and the glass, she went upstairs.

Food was some revitalizing potion. It had brought her back to life once. Maybe it could bring Teacher back just the same.

By now Teacher was almost completely quiet. She only heard occasional creaks in the floorboards letting her know he was still there. She hoped he was asleep. It would be good for him to get some sleep. She peeked into the bedroom and for a moment thought he was asleep.

Some flies were still bothering him. They had somehow gotten into the room again. They buzzed against his finger stump and even began crawling around in the wound in his forehead, but he wasn't responding to their touch. He only sat there, slumped and unmoving. He was unchanged from the last time she saw him. His whole body was limp. He was held up only by his bleeding wrists. His head was down, his chin touching his chest. His shoulders were pulling from their sockets with the weight of his own body.

When she walked into the room, his head lifted as though he sensed her presence. She couldn't tell if he had just woken up or if he had been awake the whole time.

He turned his duct taped face to her. He said nothing. He looked exhausted, weak, spent. The edges of the duct tape were peeling even more. He must have still been trying to it take it off. She wondered why he wanted to see so badly. It was still stuck on his face, still covering his eyes, but his face was so wet with all sorts of fluid. It was only a matter of time before the tape stopped sticking.

The thought of the tape sliding off his face made her skin crawl. The thought of seeing his changed face, and the thought of him seeing her. She trembled, and the food and water in her hands threatened to spill.

She hung on to her mother's words. A sick person needs to eat, her mother had said. Good food was enough to resurrect a person, bring them back to who they used to be.

Teacher would look more like himself after eating. He would get better faster. He would be Teacher again.

She stepped in front of him and felt something wet seeping into her socks. She lifted her foot and found herself standing in a puddle

Teacher was sitting in. She stifled a noise of surprise and stepped away quickly, but her sock was already soaked in it.

She wasn't entirely sure what fluid the puddle consisted of. In the TV light, she couldn't tell what color it was. It could have been many things, but it smelled strongly of urine and vomit. Vomit was one thing, but she couldn't stand the smell of urine.

She gritted her teeth. "I brought you food, Teacher," she said, and then turned red. He must have smelled the food already. There was no need to announce it.

Black drool hung from his lips in strings, almost like hair. It dripped down between his legs, adding to the puddle he sat in. He must have been vomiting still. He must have been very nauseous from that concussion. She was surprised he had anything left to vomit. His stomach must be empty by now.

She set the bowl a few centimeters away from the puddle. She clutched the glass of water in one hand, then she grabbed his chin with her free hand. Her touch made him wince, but it looked more like a twitch. It seemed he was too tired to fight against her like he had fought against her before. He only let her tilt his head back.

She tilted his head back far, as far as it would go. She looked at his mouth as his lips parted. His lips were cracked and chapped, wet only with blood and other fluids. It had been a long time since he had consumed anything. She thought he would be parched. She thought he would chug the water by the mouthful when she gave it to him.

She brought the glass to his chapped, swollen lips and began pouring the water into his mouth.

Immediately, he sputtered and spat it all out.

The water sprayed all over her. She flinched hard and stumbled backward. She couldn't stifle the noise of surprise that tore through her throat, but it was masked by the sound of Teacher's violent coughing.

"What happened?" she said, so startled and confused her voice went high.

He didn't answer. He only continued coughing hard like he was choking.

She lifted his face again and squeezed his cheeks so his mouth would open wider. She looked into his mouth, fearing it was his tongue he was choking on. But his tongue was still attached. Despite being stitched on somewhat sideways, it was still in one piece.

He wasn't choking on his tongue. Perhaps the water simply went down the wrong pipe.

"It's just water, Teacher," she clarified. Then she tried again.

She tilted his head back and poured the water into his mouth slowly this time. But the same thing happened. He choked on it as soon as it entered his mouth.

He would not swallow.

She frowned. Her confusion grew. She thought for a moment, then put the glass of water down on the floor again. She picked up the bowl of *kanom jeen*. Water didn't taste like anything. Maybe he didn't like drinking water. She didn't like drinking water either. She thought he might want to swallow if it was something that tasted good.

She gathered a small spoonful of the yellow water and some cut noodles. She brought it to his lips, but he was being resistant now. He was turning his head away. He wasn't opening his mouth for her anymore. She had to grip him by the cheeks again with one hand and squeeze the spoon through his lips with the other. His sandpaper skin scraped her palm, and the spoon clacked against his teeth. She managed to force the spoon into his mouth, but it was like she was feeding medicine to a child who didn't understand medicine would help him.

He sputtered again, more violently than he had with the water. The yellow *kanom jeen* water spewed from his mouth and sprayed all over her face. It even got into her own mouth. Strangely, it didn't even taste like *kanom jeen*. It tasted more like stale vomit and sour breath. She figured it was his mouth making the food taste different.

She was coughing now too. She grimaced and wiped her mouth on her sleeve as he leaned forward and heaved.

It really was as though he were no longer capable of swallowing.

She looked at him skeptically.

"Do you remember how to swallow, Teacher?"

He said nothing. He just kept coughing.

Her frown deepened.

How was he to get better if he couldn't swallow?

Her hands began to tremble even more. She felt a familiar fire in her, an urgency. She scooped up another spoonful of food and went for his mouth again with a sense of desperation. She only wanted him to swallow just once. Just one mouthful of food was better than nothing.

She had to force the spoon into his mouth, and as he opened his mouth to spit and sputter, she used the opportunity to force her spoon in again. As she tried to feed him, he made noises like he was drowning. Then it sounded like he was trying to speak. But every time he opened his mouth to cough or make a noise, she forced her spoon in. He kept sputtering and choking and the food kept spraying from his mouth and staining her face, her clothes, her hair. Then, with the spoon still in his mouth, he said in the gasping voice of a drowner, "You're killing me."

Though he was sputtering as he said it, it was the most clear and intelligible thing he had said thus far.

It shocked her so much she removed the spoon from his mouth. He leaned forward to cough, and then to retch.

"What did you say?" she said, still in disbelief.

He coughed but didn't repeat himself.

She had heard him clear enough the first time.

"I am not killing you," she said. She would never do that.

She wasn't trying to hurt him. All she did, she did to help him. He needed to eat, and if he could get a bit of sustenance before he vomited again, that was all right. He needed to eat just like his tongue needed to be sutured. Life was a series of doing things she didn't want to do, her mother had said. Even if those things were painful.

She tried once more. She went at his mouth again with her spoon, but before it could touch his lips he jerked his head away like he had jerked his head away from the drunk teacher who had tried to kiss him at the party. She felt her insides twist with frustration. Math class frustration. She reached for his chin again, grabbed it hard, but he still thrashed and avoided her spoon by shaking his head. She fought for his chin, and then, when she managed to force his head back up, he spat.

It landed in her eye, a thick wad of saliva, blood, and curry sauce. She was so shocked she froze over. She let go of him. She didn't know what had happened at first, only that she couldn't see out of her right eye and that it hurt. It took her a moment to fully understand what had happened.

When she did understand, she hit him.

She flew at him with the awkwardness of passion and hit his cheek with her palm. She hit him hard enough to move his head and draw a sound from him. The force of the hit threw her own body off balance too. She toppled over. She landed on her hip and caught herself on her elbow. A jolt of pain ran up her arm.

The pain was like cold water washing over her. She lay on the floor for a moment in a state of paralysis. The passion—the anger—began to dissipate, replaced slowly by the feeling of shock.

She couldn't believe she had just hit him.

She supposed it was instinct. Her mother had always told her to hit back, even if it was a man who had hurt her.

She looked up at him hesitantly. His head was down like a reprimanded child, and he was still shaking, coughing.

Slowly, she rose from the floor. She forced herself to breathe, to calm down. She sat in front of him again, right on top of the damp carpet. She wiped the hair from her face, the bloodied spit from her eye. She looked at her hand after she wiped it. Teacher's spit was thick and smelled bad. She shook it off her hand. Her eye was twitching now. It was beginning to sting. She rubbed it again. She scooped what blood and saliva she could from it, but that made it sting worse. It felt like a rock had hit it, and now her vision was blurry. She figured she needed to flush it with water. It burned so bad she almost couldn't keep it open. It was almost like he had spat acid on her.

While she couldn't believe she had hit him, she also couldn't believe he had spat on her. But she remembered the food was spicy. Her mother had dumped handfuls of chilis into it. And, as an afterthought, she remembered his tongue was injured.

It must have stung. Just like her eye now stung.

She tried to understand he must have been in a lot of pain. He must have been panicking, like a drowner pulling his savior under the water with him. She didn't even know if he had spat on her on purpose, if he had targeted his spit at her eye. Maybe he only meant to spit the food out of his mouth. Maybe it stung so bad he would do anything to get it out of his mouth. Maybe he hadn't intended for the spit to land on her at all.

She supposed they both had done things they hadn't meant to do.

She swallowed. She spoke slowly so as to steady the pitch of her voice. "Let's not do this," she said. "Let's not be like this, please."

He didn't spit again. He didn't do anything. He just sat there, breathing hard with his head still down. He seemed to understand then that whatever he did to her, she could hurt him worse. He could barely do anything to her, strung up like this. And she could do anything she wanted to do. All she needed was a will to do so.

He might have thought she had a will to hurt him.

She didn't know what to say to make him understand she never meant to hurt him. She couldn't bring herself to apologize. She couldn't explain herself either. She didn't know how to. She was never good with words.

She was silent for a long time as she thought of her next words. The silence between them was like a noise.

Finally, she opened her mouth.

"What's your favorite food, Teacher?"

The silence only returned after she finished speaking. She thought perhaps he hadn't heard her, that she had spoken too quietly. He didn't respond and she didn't want to repeat herself. She tapped him timidly on the leg and he flinched and inhaled sharply. He began mumbling in his unintelligible way and stammering as though in fear. She thought she heard him say something about *mu kratha*.

~

She could barely see. The sun was nearly setting, but it burned so brightly she had to squint her eyes. She stared at the cracked and uneven sidewalk as she walked on it. The stench of sewage rose from the cracks. She always imagined an underground river of shit flowing just beneath the concrete. She normally would have been tickled by such a thought. Now, she didn't even smile.

She had to hurry. The outdoor market would be closing soon.

Most of the vendors were packing up for the night when she reached the market. Her eye was itchy and she rubbed at it as she searched through the stalls of produce. She searched almost urgently. She tried to pick out things she thought Teacher would like. But that proved to be a bit difficult, so she based it off what she liked, figuring everyone liked *mu kratha* for the same reasons.

Soon she had plastic bags full of meat and vegetables in her hands. She began to walk home, but her eye was so itchy it began to twitch like a stomach trying to regurgitate.

It felt like something was wrong.

She hurried into a public bathroom in an alleyway. She went straight to the sink and checked her eye in the mirror.

She got a shock from seeing her reflection. She always did. She often forgot she was a person at all, and the sudden reminder was always disturbing. But this time was even more disturbing.

The sight of her eye was like a foreign object, like something she had never seen before.

Her left eyelids were enlarged, swollen, and the white part of her eye was so red it looked like it was bleeding. For a moment she thought it was Teacher's blood still in her eye. She flushed it with the sulfur-scented water from the sink. But that didn't make the redness go away. It made it look even worse. It made it itch and sting worse too.

She swallowed hard as dirty water dripped down her face. She stared at herself, at her red eye, and it was like she wasn't even looking at herself but someone else entirely. Her eye was so inflamed she forgot what it used to look like.

She left the bathroom and, after being stared at by the attendant, dropped a coin into the tip box.

~

When she returned to the attic, she found him twitching.

The sight made her pause at the bedroom doorway. He was slumped against the fishing line and twitching constantly from one thing or another. His breath hitched and his stomach convulsed with each twitch. He looked to be either heaving or climaxing. Pain and pleasure, she thought, really were indistinguishable. She supposed this was a part of him she always longed to see, a part of him she resorted to imagining, drawing. But the sight of him twitching as though from orgasm only made her think of some of the fish parts she worked with at the factory.

There were times when fish parts came to her still moving. They twitched and twisted and moved as though to get away from her knife as she cut them. Sometimes they would twitch themselves right out of her hands. Sometimes she would have to chase after them.

The factory women would laugh at the sight, the same nervous laughter they produced when they had tried out the shiny new machine. But she was always unsettled by the twitching fish. She couldn't laugh with them. She knew it was just nerve endings making the dead things dance, but she couldn't help but imagine the defiled, skinned corpses were still alive, still feeling, still conscious despite missing all their parts.

Teacher's twitching unsettled her just the same. He was like a dead thing still alive.

She fought against a shudder. She tightened her grip on the plastic grocery bags. They crinkled in her hands. The sound made him lift his head in her direction as though he could see her through the duct tape on his face.

She had to make herself enter the room.

As she approached him, she saw he was still covered in the yellow *kanom jeen*. It was all over him, like she had painted him with it instead of fed him. And as she drew closer, the bad smell of the apartment worsened.

She realized it was him who smelled. He smelled like rot and skin, like vomit and urine. She couldn't tell the difference between his stench and the attic's stench.

She was before him now and once again struck by how different he looked. His swollen face bulged around the peeling tape. The bruises on his skin had deepened. They seemed to have grown too. She didn't know bruises could grow. But it wasn't just the swelling and bruises making him change. There was something distinctly different about him now.

He looked so unlike himself.

What was it that was making him change so much? The blanching skin of his face? The yellow and green bruises growing and surfacing? Or maybe it was his nakedness making him look unlike himself. He had always dressed so piously before.

She took a breath, silent and slow. Food was some revitalizing potion, she told herself again. She almost said it aloud.

His favorite food was sure to remind him of who he was.

She put her supplies on the floor and rubbed her itchy eye. She placed an electric *mu kratha* grill right before him. It was taken from her own kitchen, used only for special occasions and celebrations. It was shiny, practically new. She and her mother rarely used it. *Mu kratha* felt wrong with just two people.

She sat cross-legged next to Teacher. She turned the grill on. She did everything she was supposed to do. She filled the crevice with water. She placed a square of fat at the rounded peak of the grill. And then she placed pieces of meat on the grill and stewed vegetables with chopsticks.

Very quickly the meat began to sizzle, the water began to steam, and an aroma began to rise. It wasn't an unpleasant aroma. At first, it was almost nice. But then it began mixing with the stench of the attic, the stench of him, and it turned into something else entirely. Something bad.

She breathed shallowly so she wouldn't have to smell it. And then the grill began to smoke. The heat the grill emitted wasn't just cooking the food. It seemed to be cooking the smell too. It made the attic even hotter, even stickier. It made the air nearly unbreathable.

She cooked hurriedly. With her chopsticks she picked up a piece of meat that looked more brown than pink. She blew on it, not wanting to burn Teacher, then pressed it to his lips. She feared his lips would remain pursed and pinched, that he would fight against her just like he did before.

She was surprised when he opened his mouth and allowed himself to be fed. The sight almost made her feel hopeful. She almost thought he would swallow. She almost thought he *wanted* to swallow. That he was eating for himself, not for her.

But she figured he was only indulging her.

It was like the last day of the term again when his students fed him *mu kratha*. She remembered the sight of him burning his mouth only to please his students and saying, "Delicious," before he even had time to register its taste.

Now he opened his mouth for her just the same. Or perhaps he opened his mouth like he had opened his mouth for her needle. To make way for it so it wouldn't hurt him.

She pursed her lips. She inserted the meat into his mouth and dropped it inside. She watched him hard as he moved the piece of meat around in his mouth. He chewed on it for a long time. He looked like he was struggling. His jaw moved strangely, like he had forgotten how to chew just as he had forgotten how to swallow. And then, suddenly, he stopped chewing altogether.

He let the meat just sit in his mouth. His lips twitched uneasily, like he was afraid.

"What?" she said, confused.

"Teeth," he said.

"Teeth?"

"Loose."

"Your teeth are loose?"

He nodded his head.

Her face twisted. "Still?" she said.

Were more teeth going to fall out? Had she beaten him with her hammer that hard? Or was he starting to fall apart on his own?

She reached a hand toward him. When she touched his mouth he flinched. It was starting to annoy her how he flinched every time she made a sound or touched him. He responded to her touch like she meant to hurt him every time.

She quickly inserted her fingers into his mouth and plucked the meat out. She examined the meat. She pinched it between her fingers and squeezed the juices out of it. She couldn't tell if it was his juices or the meat's. The piece was a bit thick. Maybe too thick for him to chew with loose teeth. And it was pink on the inside. It was probably too raw, too tough.

She let the wad of meat fall to the floor.

She took another piece of meat off the grill and tried it herself. The meat was still a bit tough, she thought, but not too tough. She thought maybe she could chew it for him.

She continued to chew. The taste filled her mouth. It wasn't a bad taste. But it soon began to evolve. With the attic's smell and his smell invading her nostrils, it was making the meat taste bad.

She felt her throat constrict. She knew she would gag if she tried to swallow.

She spat the meat out promptly. She tried to eat a piece of a vegetable then, but even the vegetables tasted like flesh. She grabbed a spoon and tried the broth. She burned her mouth in her haste to try it. Still, she found everything tasted the same. Everything tasted like how the attic smelled. How Teacher now smelled.

She looked down at the grill, all the meat and vegetables sizzling, water bubbling, and she thought about what a waste it all was. She couldn't eat anything. She had no appetite in this room. And Teacher couldn't eat when his teeth were loose.

Soon the meat would start to blacken and burn on the grill.

Her throat began to constrict even further. It began hurting so much she was about to cry. She hated crying just like she hated peeing. Crying only brought attention to oneself.

She frantically sought a way to distract herself. She picked the half-cooked meat off the grill with her chopsticks and began sticking them onto the nearby wall. She busied herself with lining them up properly, sticking them on the wall straight and putting the pieces in order from tallest to shortest. It was a great distraction, like a puzzle.

He started trying to talk to her again. She felt bubbling in her chest. The sound of the water bubbling, too, made it feel like her heart was boiling in her ribcage. She tried to ignore him, but when he was blinded, her silence seemed to make him think she couldn't hear him, to which he would get louder.

He sounded even worse than before. His strange accent had thickened, and it was all the more apparent when he yelled.

"What?" she said. She sounded snappish. She only wanted him to quiet down.

"Name," he said.

She paused her sticking and turned to look at him. "What about it?"

"Name," he only repeated.

"I'm not telling you my name," she said. "So stop asking."

She turned back to the meat on the wall. She found her language was changing too. Her tongue was growing sharp. It was like she wasn't talking to a teacher, but a peer.

"Dear?" he said then.

"That's not my name," she spat.

His lips pinched. She stuck another piece on the wall.

"Aoey?" he said.

"That's not it, either."

"Pear?"

"No."

"Nam?"

"Stop," she said, snapping her head to look at him again. If he was going through them all, he might actually get to hers. "No more."

His lips pinched again.

"Why do you want to know my name so badly?" she muttered.

"Friends," he said.

"We're not friends," she said. "I don't want to be your friend. Be quiet now, please."

He was quiet then, but his lips were pursing, quivering, like he was chewing on them. She knew from knowing him that he did this when he was thinking. He was contemplating something right now. She didn't know what was going on inside his head. Her stomach felt cold again and she realized she was afraid of what he was thinking. She shifted uncomfortably on the floor. She stopped sticking the meat on the walls. She let the rest of the meat burn on the grill. It began smoking badly. It made her eyes sting. Her infected eye began twitching again, yet she could do nothing but stare at his head as though she could crack his skull and see inside it if she stared hard enough.

Suddenly, he turned his head toward her, always as though he could see her through the duct tape. He looked at her in resignation.

"Love," he said.

Her brow creased. "Pardon?" she said.

"Love."

Her face burned. "I don't understand what you're saying," she said.

"Love me," he said.

He was still trying to understand. She did love him, but this was not just a crush. This was so much more than a crush. But how was she to explain?

"It's not like that," she said.

"Love me," he said again. And she realized then it wasn't a question.

He wasn't asking for confirmation. He was saying *love* like how a hostage says *money*.

She couldn't speak for a moment. Her throat constricted so tight she couldn't even breathe. She had to force the words out and they came out squeaky and weak. "I don't understand," she said. She knew she could get out of things by feigning ignorance.

But he wouldn't stop.

"Love," he said again.

"No, I don't know what you're saying." She had an idea of what he was saying.

"*Love*," he said. The more she refused him the more adamant he became, like he knew she knew what he meant, like he wouldn't let her pretend otherwise. "Love. Love. Love—"

"*Stop it.*"

It came out louder than she had intended. It made them both wince, and then shut up. They sat without talking. The only sound was of the meat still sizzling on the grill. She looked at it and saw the meat shriveling and blackening. The water in the pot had steamed itself into nothing. There was nothing left to eat.

Tears stung her throat.

She only wanted him in a place where she could always see him. She wasn't prepared for how much he would see of her.

"I really don't want to talk to you right now," she said as evenly as she could. And then she turned around so she could sit with her back facing him. She didn't want to look at him right now either. She needed a moment away from everything. When things got too much for her, she needed to remove herself for a while, and then when she returned she would be calmer, more in control of herself. She learned that after the incident in the math class.

She now felt frustration not unlike the one she felt in that math class. It was a type of frustration that felt like it would never dissipate. It felt like it had to burst in order to be relieved. She felt like it would burst right now like it had burst before. She was about to rise from the floor and remove herself from the room completely before anything could burst, but a sudden sound made her freeze.

It came from behind her. A wet, sticky sound.

She thought at first it was the sound of Teacher trying to peel the duct tape off his face. But the sound was softer than duct tape. It almost sounded like how the fish parts sounded when she tore them apart at the factory. But it was warmer, if a sound could be warm.

Slowly, fearfully, she looked over her shoulder at Teacher.

At once, her stomach surged with nausea.

She saw him yanking very hard yet very calmly at his bound wrists. It looked like he was aggressively scratching an itch.

"What are you doing?" she hissed.

But she already knew he wasn't itching himself. He was cutting himself.

It didn't look like he was trying to wring his hands loose like he had been doing before. It looked more like he was sawing at his wrists. Already he had degloved a large portion of his left wrist. The more he worked at it, the tighter the fishing line got. His face beneath the tape was twisted with a look of pain or concentration. He didn't respond to her question. He didn't even acknowledge she was in the room. He just kept cutting.

"*Stop it*," she hissed again, and she grabbed his wrists to keep them still. They were warm and slippery with blood. She couldn't get a firm grasp on them, so she couldn't make him still. He kept moving his wrists against her, and his blood was like lubricant. He was stronger than her, even strung up and injured like this. She hung onto him and he was moving her too. She swayed with each sawing motion he made. It was making her sick. She let go of him. Trying to stop him was like trying to stop a locomotive with her hands when she should have been searching for an off switch.

All the while the line kept slicing through his skin like meat.

"You won't amputate yourself," she said. He must have been trying to amputate himself, trying to escape any way he could. "The line can't cut through bone. Stop it."

But he didn't stop.

The squelching sound was awful and it somehow seemed to be getting louder, deeper. It sounded like it was inside her head. It sounded like her own brain was squelching inside her skull. It was louder than the sound of sizzling meat. It was louder than anything.

"Stop it!" she kept saying, but he wouldn't, and so, not knowing what else to do, she burst.

She flung the grill at him.

The sound of loud sizzling erupted, like meat thrown into an oiled pan. The grill collided with his abdomen, scalded the flesh there before falling face down atop his right thigh. The bulging top of the grill burned into the skin of his thigh. Smoke rose, thicker than the smoke of the pork. He screamed as he attempted to shake the grill from him, but he could barely move, strung up as he was.

It was she who moved the grill away eventually. But she couldn't apologize. She was still too upset.

~

She had been given everything she wanted as a child, mostly to make up for almost being dead at three years old. She didn't want much, so her mother began giving her things she thought she would like. She was often gifted small pets. Her mother knew her well enough to know she did not desire friendship. Her mother respected this part of her and never forced her to socialize, not even with family. Her mother must have thought pets were decent enough company.

The landlord didn't allow pets, but he was never one to enforce or check. Small things that couldn't make noise to disturb the neighbors were fine. Like fish. They had plenty of pet fish. They didn't do much and they didn't make any noise. She thought they were nice to look at for a while, but they weren't supposed to be touched. She couldn't even hold them. She would often stick her hands in their tanks just to pet them, but they would always dart away from her, and the feeling of them didn't give her much satisfaction.

To her, the prospect of getting a pet was always better than actually having one.

When she was sick of fish her mother gave her a bird. But birds were too noisy. They were kind of creepy too. That bird had chewed its own foot off and then died. It was kind of a relief when it died. Both she and her mother had been too creeped out by it to care for it properly anyway.

She remembered that bird now. She remembered how it looked when it chewed off its foot.

In her head she could still hear the sound of Teacher in the attic, sawing at his own wrist as though to cut his hand off.

~

"It still stinks in here," her mother said.

She said nothing. She lay on the couch, watching her mother arrange bouquets of flowers around the apartment.

They kept flowers in their apartment sometimes. Since they

worked at the factory, the smell of fish tended to follow them and stink up the apartment. The flowers masked the smell of fish, and they looked nice too.

Her mother said, "You'd think that after they took the corpse away it would start smelling better. Why the hell is it getting worse?"

Her mother placed a bouquet on the coffee table in front of her. She reached out lazily and plucked out a flower. It was a nice blue flower, but when she held it to her nose and inhaled, she still only smelled rotten meat.

They always got the flowers from the flower shop down the street. It was the same streetside garage she had stolen the flatbed cart from in her acquisition of Teacher. The flower shop owner gave her and her mother discounted prices on the flowers. It was because he had known her when she was a sick child. At one point she had been so sick her mother planned for her funeral. Being friends, the flower man had supplied her with dozens of funeral flowers free of charge.

But then she hadn't died. Things were a bit awkward between them and the flower man ever since. Still, out of courtesy or obligation or apology, the flower man continued to give them discounted prices on flowers. They never mentioned the funeral thing.

Her mother was sniffing the air now.

"It almost smells like meat." She laughed a bit. "Why does it smell like *mu kratha*? Now I'm kind of hungry." Then she laughed so hard she had to cross her legs.

She didn't laugh along with her mother though. She knew the smell was coming from Teacher. She couldn't forget it when he was moaning like he was moaning right now.

She didn't go to him for a long time after burning him, perhaps two full days. She had lost track of time. It was easy for her to lose track of time. And ever since then he had been moaning constantly. It almost sounded like a frequency. There was no pause in it, no break. It made the entire apartment throb. It was like a part of the building now. She wondered if she was actually hearing it or if she had grown accustomed to hearing it that she kept hearing it.

Suddenly her mother, who never heard anything, looked up at the ceiling.

"What is that?" her mother said.

She felt a shock to her chest like electricity. "You heard that?"

"I felt it," her mother said. "Is there something in the attic?"

She couldn't speak. She managed to shrug.

Her mother frowned and then mumbled to herself something about ghosts in the attic.

~

She put one of Teacher's teeth in her mouth again. She sucked hard at the tooth, trying to suck anything she could out of it. She turned it over in her mouth with her tongue like a nervous tic. And then she made her way up the stairs to the attic.

She opened the bedroom door slowly, timidly. She poked her head inside.

Immediately, she felt a jolt of terror when she saw him.

He was as she left him, hanging from the ceiling by his bleeding wrists, legs folded underneath him like a child. That much was unchanged. But scarcely anything else was the same.

He didn't look like a human. He looked more like lumps of flesh barely held together by string.

She couldn't see the details of him, only colors and lumps. But his abdomen and leg looked like they had the texture of shredded meat.

His twitching from before had turned into shivering. He shivered so hard his teeth chattered and he made noises like he was cold. She couldn't understand it at first. It wasn't cold in this room. It was stuffy and hot, and he was covered in a sheen of sweat. It looked like someone had dumped a bucket of water on him.

The duct tape had finally given in. It was no longer around his eyes. It was soggy and barely clinging to his nose now. It seemed he had cried, bled, sweated the duct tape off his face.

She watched him for a long time. She watched him change colors every few seconds from the TV light. She forced herself to move. She passed all the remnants of what she had left behind. The plastic bags were everywhere, once full of vegetables and meat from the outdoor market, now empty like shed skin. The grill was on the floor where she had left it. It had bits of meat still stuck on it. She didn't know if bits of him were on there too. And the strips of pork were still stuck on the walls, lined up carefully by her own hands. The flies swarmed the meat instead of him now.

The floorboards creaked under her feet, but he didn't even look up at her. It was like he didn't even hear her. He just kept shivering. She looked at his forehead as she approached him. The wound there looked like a shiny open mouth, the bone peeking out like a tooth. When she got closer, she saw it wasn't sweat he dripped with. It was the fluid from the wound.

CUTE AGGRESSION

The wound no longer bled. It wept that indistinguishable, clear, sour-smelling fluid, like some sort of ectoplasm. Like his soul was leaking right out of him. She didn't know how he could leak so much fluid. She feared he would deflate. She feared she would have nothing left of him.

She crouched before him carefully. If he knew she was there, he made no sign. He just kept shivering and shuddering like he was freezing to death. She realized that even without the duct tape over his eyes, he still couldn't see. If the pain was bad enough to make him shiver, it was bad enough to blind him too. He didn't care to see things when shivering with pain.

She looked down at his burns. She could see them more clearly up close like this, but the proximity somehow made the burns look less real. It didn't even look like skin anymore. She didn't think the human body could ever look like this. She had thought his burnt skin would just be red, like a bad sunburn. Perhaps there would be grill marks branding him. But his burnt leg and abdomen looked diseased. They bubbled with yellow blisters. They were all sorts of colors, and they were very shiny. In some places it looked like the skin was melted. In other places his skin looked like shredded meat, or perhaps peeling tree bark. The burn in his leg looked about to burst. It looked strangely soft. It bulged outward, like it was full of fluid. It looked like the biggest pimple.

Curiously, she brought her fingers to it. She touched it carefully, but as soon as she pressed her two fingers to it, her fingers simply sank right into him.

She cried out at the same time he did. The tooth almost flew right out of her mouth.

Her fingers sank very deep. They sank right into him, and he screamed as though she had burned him all over again. She snatched her hand out of him immediately, but he was still screaming. It was a terrible sound, and so loud. More like an animal than a human. He didn't look human, and he certainly didn't sound human. She couldn't bear the sound. She lunged forward and covered his mouth with her hand, the same one that had been in his leg. She shushed him, desperately hissing at him through her teeth. He was crying under her hand and shivering even more, but he quieted down a bit. Perhaps he couldn't be loud even if he wanted to with her hand over his mouth.

The skin of his face was so hard against her hand. It was almost like plastic. She knew it was the swelling making him hard. The swelling wasn't going down like she thought it would. It seemed to only get worse with time.

His eyes were squeezed shut, or perhaps they were too swollen to open. His skin was also slimy with leaking fluids. She watched his forehead wound weep right onto her hand. The wound seemed to have gotten bigger somehow. She could see the clumps of scabs attempting and failing to form. The wound couldn't scab over when it was leaking like that.

She looked down at his burns again. She thought they would go down the same path. They would try to heal themselves, but all their progress would be washed away.

These weren't wounds that got better on their own.

They only got worse and bigger. They would keep getting bigger until they were all over him.

His whole body would be one big wound, crusting and weeping at the same time.

She needed to help him. He couldn't help himself.

"I'm going to help you, okay?" she said in the same urgent hissing tone she had when she shushed him.

He didn't nod. He didn't try to speak. He didn't even open his eyes. He only sniveled against her hand.

She took her hand away from him, and it came away with stringy fluids, perhaps snot. She grimaced and promptly wiped her hand on her pants. Then she rose. She left the bedroom and went straight to the bathroom where the medicine cabinet was. Compared to the stench of Teacher, the bathroom almost smelled nice.

She looked through the medicine cabinet above the sink. She had seen many medicine tubes and bottles when she had searched here days prior. She figured old people were accustomed to falling apart. There had to be something here that would help Teacher.

Her hands shook as she sifted through the tubes and bottles. She squinted at them to read their names. She didn't find any burn cream, but she found one half-empty tube of hemorrhoid cream.

She figured hemorrhoids weren't all that different from burns. It was all just broken skin at the end of the day. She might even be able to use it on his cuts and wounds too.

She grabbed the tube, then grabbed some packs of pain and fever pills. Teacher shivered and sweated like he had a fever, and he must be in a lot of pain. He would eat them like candy.

She ran back to Teacher. She nearly tripped over herself in her haste. She kneeled before him again. She reached for him and peeled the duct tape and the blindfold off his face. They slipped right off.

She saw the roll of duct tape still on the floor near Teacher. She felt an urge to wrap more tape over his eyes, but what point was there in blinding him again? Nothing would stick to him with his forehead weeping like that, and he was shivering too hard to look at her.

His forehead wound kept weeping that clear, sour-smelling fluid. It ran down his face, mixing with his blood. In the TV light, the blood and fluid mixture looked bright pink, like fake movie blood.

She examined his other wounds. His wrists were even more torn than before. The blood on his arms was fresh. She knew he must have been sawing at his wrists the entire time she was gone. She could hear it in her head again, the sound of him slicing his own skin. She could see it in her head too. Just like that ugly old bird chewing off its own foot.

She shuddered almost as hard as he was shuddering. She fumbled with the tube of cream, squeezed out a palmful of the stuff. It was thick and faintly yellow, like animal fat. She brought it to his burnt leg. She thought he would find relief in it, but as soon as she touched him he began screaming again, that terrible, animalistic scream.

She jumped hard. She looked down at his leg and saw that as she was rubbing the ointment in, his burnt skin was just falling apart.

But perhaps it was necessary, she thought. If the skin was falling apart, it was already dead. Maybe she needed to clear away the dead skin to make way for the new skin. Maybe it was like exfoliation.

She rubbed harder, but he cried harder. He began hyperventilating like she was torturing him instead of helping him. And when she looked down at his leg she saw she had wiped more than a layer of dead skin away. She had rubbed entire chunks of flesh off him.

She retracted her hand, and the chunks of flesh were sticking to her palm. She looked down and could see the pink and red of the inside of his leg. She was looking *inside* him, she realized.

She felt a sudden bout of heat on her face, so intense it made her head swim. It felt like her skull was burning inside her.

There was something intimate about the insides. It was like he was opening himself up to her.

She shook the chunks of flesh off her hand. They landed with a slapping sound onto the carpet.

She squeezed more ointment onto her hand. She was gentler with the burns on his abdomen, but he still cried and hyperventilated. It sounded like he was choking on his own breath. And his eyes flitted about wildly in his head. They didn't focus on anything. They were open, but she knew they were unseeing.

As she rubbed the ointment onto his stomach, she figured out too late she should have cleaned the wounds first. She found bits of *mu kratha* meat still stuck on him. The burns had made the meat stick to him.

She flicked a piece of pork away with her fingers. Some of his skin came off with it.

She realized she couldn't tell the difference between him and the pork.

She felt a pressure in her stomach, almost like someone had kicked her. She took her hands away from him. He shivered so hard it made the peeling, burnt skin shake like tassels in the wind. Like feathers.

Do things this bad ever heal? she wondered.

Maybe there was no way to heal it. Maybe the only thing that could be done was ease the pain. She had gotten to that point before. She had gotten so sick there was no medicine in the world that could save her, so the doctors pumped her full of pain pills instead. If they couldn't heal her, they could numb her. It might have made her sicker, but that didn't matter anymore. There came a point when nothing mattered anymore.

She traded the tube of ointment for a pack of pain and fever pills. She picked one out and forced the medicine into him. He didn't spit it out, but he didn't swallow it either. It was like a pacifier in his mouth, and he shuddered and hiccupped instead of crying. She remembered he couldn't swallow for some reason. But he didn't need to swallow. He just needed it to dissolve on his tongue. It would enter his bloodstream that way. When she was a sick girl, the pills were often too big, too adult for her throat. Her mother taught her to let it dissolve.

"Better, right?" she said.

He opened his mouth. She thought perhaps he would speak. But then he began vomiting.

Was it still his concussion making him vomit? Or could pain itself make someone vomit? Or was something else wrong with him? Was his stomach shutting down? Was all of him shutting down?

He vomited all over himself again. It got all over his wounds, his burns. It must have felt like acid, and she couldn't even clean it up for fear of more of his skin coming off into her hands.

CUTE AGGRESSION

She couldn't stop looking at him, for reasons so different from before. He was so exposed. His body was full of holes. His insides were spilling out. It wasn't awe that kept her staring. It wasn't his beauty, like sublime nature that kept her in an awe-stricken state. It was how unsightly he had become.

He was something horrific she couldn't look away from.

Things this bad didn't heal, she knew.

This was something he might not come back from.

She couldn't plug his wounds. She couldn't wrap them or wipe them. She couldn't touch him without him falling apart in her hands. She couldn't make him look any better. She couldn't make him more like himself. Every attempt would be flushed right away by his leaking wounds. Every attempt would just make him fall apart even more.

But was that all she loved him for? His appearance?

Was her love for him that shallow?

That couldn't be, she thought. He was her whole world. He was all the thoughts in her head. A girl couldn't love a man that much just for his looks. She loved him for who he was. He was special. He had to be special or else she could never have orbited around him like she had for years.

His outsides may have been ruined. She couldn't fix him on the outside. But maybe she could fix his insides.

~

Pleng luk thung. Old country music was what Teacher liked to listen to. An old soul, people at school would call him. They would laugh at a young man playing such old music in his classroom as his students left or walked in. It showed his insides didn't match his outsides, and it made him all the more endearing.

If food couldn't resurrect him, maybe music could.

She found a small radio in the old lady's apartment. She knew the old lady had a radio. She had often heard the music it played through the floorboards before the old lady died. She searched for it and found it in the living room. It was a small, archaic thing with a long antenna like an insect's.

She then sifted through Teacher's little white cassette tapes still on the bedroom floor. She chose one at random. She put the cassette into the machine and pressed play.

She thought the machine was broken at first. The noise it emitted sounded like its metal insides were grinding and squealing. But she then realized the noise was only the song. The radio was so old it

118

made the music it played sound even older than it was. It made it sound sharper too. Metallic, like the intercom at school, she thought. The voice on the tape was a pretty voice, but the machine made it sound piercing. It sounded nothing like it would have sounded in his classroom.

If Teacher noticed the difference, he made no indication. He made no indication he even heard the song at all.

"Teacher," she said, "do you know this song?"

He didn't respond. He just kept shivering.

She felt a burst of fear in her chest and thought for a moment he was suddenly incapable of hearing just like he was incapable of talking, of swallowing.

She picked up the radio and held it close to Teacher's ear. Immediately, he recoiled, and she saw a wince run through his swollen face.

The fear in her began to melt, but some remnants remained. He responded to its sound like it wasn't music at all, just noise.

She set the radio back down on the floor. She figured it would take some time for the music to fill his ears and work its way into his brain. Once it marinated in his brain, would it remind him of himself?

She looked at all the belongings scattered on the floor. Her eyes locked onto one of the history books. She recognized its cover. They had used this book when she was in his class. She picked it up. It was worn from use. He had been using it for his classes for many years.

The tattered pages looked like the peeling, burnt skin of his abdomen. She cringed as she flipped through them.

She thought it a good idea to read a history book to him to help remind him of himself. But as she leafed through the pages and scanned the contents, she felt a sinking feeling. The language was too hard for her to understand. It must have been too hard for Teacher now, too, with his head bashed as it was. He couldn't even pronounce words correctly now. Could he even process words the same way he used to?

Would he even remember the book if she read it to him?

Had she knocked all the history right out of his head?

With a shudder she dropped the book to the floor. It landed on top of another book. A book with a familiar chicken on the cover.

Carefully, she reached under the history book and picked up the children's alphabet book.

Maybe she should start from the beginning, she thought. Lay out the foundation and build him up from there.

CUTE AGGRESSION

She sat cross-legged before him. The floor creaked so loudly as she settled down, it drowned out the tinny music.

Teacher didn't look up at her. It was like he didn't even know she was there.

She opened the children's book to the first page. She held it out for him to see, but he still wasn't looking up.

She reached out and timidly tapped him on the cheek. He winced the same way he winced when she held the radio to his ear, then he looked up. With his eyes so swollen, she couldn't tell if he was looking at her or at the book.

"Teacher," she said, pointing to the page, "what is this consonant?"

He kept shivering. His teeth started chattering again.

"*Gaw-gai*," she said. C for chicken. "Can you say it? *Gaw-gai*."

He couldn't seem to concentrate. His head began dropping down again. Her hand darted out and tapped him on the leg close to his burns to get his attention. He didn't respond to her touch. It seemed he didn't have feeling in his leg anymore.

She tapped his cheek again instead. He twitched, then looked fleetingly at the book held before his face.

He seemed to understand what she wanted.

He opened his mouth. She waited for him to utter the words, but it was taking so long, and the waiting was making her eye itch, then twitch.

"*Gaw-gai*," she said again. She pronounced it as well as she could, but her voice shook with impatience. She found herself getting frustrated as she waited for him to repeat after her. She rubbed hard at her eye. His mouth looked to be attempting to form the words, but nothing was coming out.

"I heard you say a whole sentence the other day," she said. "'You're killing me,' you said. You can say that, but not *gaw-gai*?"

Some sounds came out of his mouth then. They were unintelligible. They sounded nothing like *gaw-gai*. He couldn't speak well through chattering teeth, and his throat was spasming and constricting too much, making it hard for him to get anything out.

She stifled a sigh. She turned the page. She held it out for him.

"*Kaw-kuat*," she said. B for bottle.

He muttered something. It didn't even sound like words.

This wasn't helping him. It was making him sound more stupid, more unlike himself.

120

"This isn't you, Teacher," she said. "*Kaw-kuat.*"

As he tried to indulge her, drool began spilling from his open mouth. It was viscous and red. He was still bleeding so much from the mouth. She couldn't understand how he still had so much blood left in him. She wondered where it was coming from. His tongue, his gums. Maybe from his insides. Maybe he was breaking down on the inside.

The blood made his words sound wet, and the sound of it grated her ears. She paused her teaching to sop up the blood in his mouth with her sleeve. But his mouth was just like the wound on his forehead. It just kept leaking no matter how much she wiped it.

Where was her teacher in all this mess? She couldn't find a trace of him. It was like he was never there.

She kept wiping, but he kept spilling. Parts of him falling out, collecting in the fabric of her shirt. She wiped hard, but the skin of his face didn't even bow. It was too swollen. His face didn't even feel like a face. His lips didn't feel like lips. They felt hard and inanimate. And when she felt them moving beneath her arm, a jolt of fear like electricity made her snatch her arm away from him.

It was like a dead thing coming alive. But she realized he was moving his mouth because he was trying to talk again.

He wasn't trying to repeat after her. He wasn't trying to pronounce the Thai alphabet. A long string of unintelligible words came from his lips. He was trying to talk to her, but he sounded like a cow again. He sounded like he was mooing at her.

The frustration in her felt sharp, like a knife cutting her from the inside, clawing its way out.

"No, no," she said quickly, shaking her head hard, making the hair fly off her forehead. "I'm not talking to you if you're going to sound like that."

But he wasn't listening to her. He kept trying to say something. It was like his life depended on it. He sounded worse than before. When he spoke, she could hear his mangled tongue, his missing teeth, his bashed head.

How could he sound like he used to sound? In class he was so eloquent, even his nervous stammer sounded articulate. But now he sounded like an idiot. It made tears sting in her eyes and in her throat. He was so far from himself.

"Let down, please," he said finally.

She sighed very hard, like a frustrated buffalo.

"Let down, please."

She sucked her teeth. "You said that already."

"Dying," he said.

"You are not dying," she said.

"Dying."

"Teacher."

"*Dying.*"

"*Teacher!*"

As she screamed it, his tooth flew from her mouth.

It was a small thing, but it landed on the floor with a noise loud enough to silence both of them.

Both their heads turned to look at it as it rolled around the floor like a marble. She scurried to pick it back up. But he saw it. He looked at her unblinkingly as she put it in her pocket.

She felt the skin of her face burn. Her chest filled with bubbles of frustration.

"What?" she spat as he looked at her.

She felt like she was going to cry. Her face contorted, and she thought she really would cry.

She covered her face with her hands, but she could feel his eyes on her still and she could feel the warmth of her own embarrassed skin. Her face felt so hot she thought her skin would melt off. It was like he was burning her with his gaze. She desperately wished he were unseeing. She wished he'd stop looking at her, thinking things about her.

When the warmth was too much to handle, she flung her hands away from her face.

She lunged for a plastic grocery bag on the floor. It was still wet and pink with blood from the meat. The sound it made as she clutched it in her hands was like TV static.

She ran behind Teacher. She put it over his head. She pulled the ends hard against his neck.

The realization of what she meant to do seemed to resurrect him.

He came alive again. He thrashed hard, shaking his head like a dog, like he meant to shake her off him. She clung to him harder, still burning with embarrassment. She tightened her grip on the bag. He was trying to breathe, but soon there was no air left in the bag, only plastic, and he sucked the pink plastic into his open mouth and stained it red.

He grew weak against her. Instead of fighting and wrestling him, it felt like she was hugging him. She was flat against his back, like that first night. And soon he was asleep, like that first night.

It was silent now except for the crinkling of the plastic bag.

He was very still in her arms.

She didn't know how long she held him like that. Her chin rested on his shoulder. She stayed put until her own breathing slowed and her own frustration quelled. Her hair stuck to her face with sweat, but she was cooling down now. Her face was no longer hot enough to melt. She felt better.

All she needed was a little quiet, a little stillness.

"That's better, Teacher," she said, panting softly.

She turned her head slightly, pivoting her chin on his shoulder, and looked at his face. He was blurry beneath the plastic. He looked like a series of colors. She could see the shapes of him, but no details. He was unconscious and suddenly he was her teacher again.

She felt the twist of affection in her guts.

She pressed her cheek against his. The bag crinkled. She liked him like this. When he couldn't see her or feel her on him. It was like a redo of the night she had acquired him. Things only started going wrong after he woke up. If only there was a way to keep him like this always.

Amid the stillness, she realized her grip on the bag had never loosened. It was still tight around his neck. She loosened her fingers and leaned on him.

She felt him breathe against her. The bag made loud crinkling noises, like static again. He was stirring. He was groaning. He was making ugly cow sounds again, and he was moving against her. It was horrific, like some doll come to life. And as he was coming to life it felt like something was slipping away from her.

Hastily, she tightened the bag around his throat again. She pulled so hard the bag stretched. She kept pulling until he stopped making noises, until he became still again, until it was silent except for the sound of dripping.

This time when she took the bag off, he didn't stir.

She tossed the bag away. It floated in the air like a jellyfish in water. It slowly descended to the floor and settled there, flattening with gravity. When the crinkling stopped, the room was quiet again.

The quiet was so serene. It could make any bad smell become good.

She clung to him like this for a long time. She didn't look at him, she only felt him. She shut her eyes tight and touched his body. Without seeing it, his body felt nice. His wounds felt soothingly warm. If she didn't look at them, they felt all right.

With her eyes still closed she laid her head on his leg.

The burns there made the softest pillow.

~

She was disturbed awake by the TV flashing.

It flashed so brightly she felt her pupils constrict painfully fast beneath her closed eyelids, and she could see its white light even with her eyes closed.

She tried to open her eyes but only one of them opened. The other one, the infected one, felt like it was glued shut. She reached up and peeled it open. It stung badly as she did so. The infection fluids made her eyelids stick together. It was like they were taped shut.

When both her eyes were open, she looked at the TV, but she found it was no longer flashing. It was calm and dim and green. It was playing a farming program again.

She wondered if it had ever been flashing at all. Maybe it was a dream.

She rose from where she lay, but she felt stuck. Her cheek felt like it was plastered to something, just like her eyelids were stuck over her infected eye. She realized her cheek was glued to the burnt skin of his leg where she had fallen asleep. She had to peel her cheek free, and as she did so, parts of Teacher came off with her, still stuck on her cheek.

She rubbed at the parts of him stuck on her cheek. When she sat up, her body began tingling. Her nerves were slowly coming back to life, bringing her back to reality. And as she was slowly made aware of her body again, she realized she was wet.

It felt like she had just gotten out of the shower. She brought her own damp knee to her nose and sniffed. It smelled like piss and for a horrible moment she thought she had pissed herself in her sleep. She soon realized it was Teacher's urine she was wet with. Teacher must have urinated when she suffocated him.

She was surprised he had enough fluid in his body left to urinate. The smell of urine rose from him and its stench was like a familiar bad dream. Like that bad time in math class.

Even if it wasn't her piss, the smell and feeling of it remained unpleasant. She figured everyone's urine was the same.

She frowned and looked at Teacher under the calm green TV light as she stretched the sleep out of her joints. He was the same as he was when she had fallen asleep on him. He was still limp. His chin was still touching his chest. He was still held up only by the fishing line like some marionette doll. She didn't know how long he had been this way. She didn't know how long she had been asleep.

She reached out and tapped his cheek.

"Teacher," she said.

He didn't stir. He didn't even twitch. He was so still, and it was so different from his shivering and shuddering from before. It was almost like he was dead.

She felt cold suddenly.

Was he dead?

She looked at his stomach and chest and couldn't detect any movement, any indication of breath.

She tapped his cheek again, harder.

"Teacher," she said in a louder voice. It was perhaps the loudest she had ever spoken to him. But he still made no response.

Could she have killed him?

"*Teacher.*" She tapped his cheek so hard it was practically a slap.

He moved then and a surge of hope nearly made her piss herself. But she realized it was only her slap moving him and making his burnt skin jiggle.

Panic began to flood her.

There were limits to the human body. It was just meat after all. Once meat began to rot, there was no way to reverse it. There was no bringing it back. If he was dead, he would soon be as cold and waxy as his finger had been before she tossed it into the machine.

She kept hitting his cheek, kept shouting his name in his ear, but to no avail. She remembered then he had woken up vomiting the first night, so she stuck her fingers far down his throat. She kept pushing. She pushed as far as her hand would go, then tried to push further.

Suddenly, it felt like she was being sucked inside him. It was like he was eating her. She felt her fingers being pulled down his throat by a wind-like force. She made a startled noise and tried pulling her hand out of him. And then she felt sharp pressure on her hand.

Teacher was biting down on her.

The pulling feeling intensified and she realized the wind-like force was his breath. He was trying to breathe. He was coming back. He was waking up biting and swallowing.

She yanked her hand from him hard and his teeth scraped against her skin. They felt like little nails scratching her. As she yanked her hand out, he began coughing instead of sucking. It sounded like he was choking even with her hand no longer there to choke him with. And then he made horrible gasping noises, like there was some metal whistle in his throat. At the same time he began moving his body again. He moved like he didn't know he was bound. It was like he was waking up in the attic for the first time all over again.

She knew he must have felt like how she had felt when she woke up. She knew his nerves were coming back to life. She knew he was becoming aware of his body again. It would take some time to come back to reality.

But the more he came back to himself, the more apparent it was that something was wrong.

He began twitching.

It was a different kind of twitch from before. It looked like little bursts of electricity were coursing through his body. With each burst he would contort his face and tense his body. It was like he was one great muscle spasming. His eyes had gone wide, just like an animal's, rolling around in his skull, confused yet aware at the same time.

She met those eyes. It was just like meeting eyes with a dog and not knowing what it was thinking, how it was thinking, if it was even capable of thinking.

~

She shoved her hand under her mattress. She felt her bloodstained school shirt. She felt his hard little teeth—only three of them now. She felt the tattered cover of her sketchbook, tattered like his burnt skin was tattered.

She grabbed the book, nearly tearing it in her haste to get it out.

She flipped through it and looked at all the drawings she had made of him.

They were terrible drawings. They looked like a child had drawn them, though she had earnestly tried. There was none of his likeness though. She could never capture his likeness.

The very first drawing was a simple portrait of him in class. It was crude and childish, but it was the start of everything. It was drawn by her twelve-year-old hand. It was now faded with time. Looking at it made her want to go back to that classroom. She wanted to be twelve years old again. She wanted him to be as he was again, walking into class looking like a youth, like a student, like a military man, like a teacher.

But would he ever be as he was again?

The suffocation seemed to have damaged his brain even more than her hammer blows had. His brain was so damaged he might as well have been dead. Flipping through the book, it really was like he was dead.

She turned a few pages. On this spread he was kicking a *takraw* ball.

Did he ever even play *takraw* outside of the classroom? Was that only something he did to please his students?

She flipped a few more pages and he was kissing someone. A man or a woman, she couldn't tell.

The next page, he was on a horse, in war. That was when she had started imagining him in the stories he told. From then on she would imagine him in every story she heard.

She turned the page. Her fingers clawed into the paper, making a dent, nearly tearing it. On the next page she saw him being raped.

She hadn't known what a penis looked like when she had drawn it. She had drawn it like a big stick. But now she knew what they looked like in real life. Little pieces of meat, dangling.

She flipped to the last drawing she had made. It was the one made in math class only a few days ago. The one with him naked. Bent over. There were no more drawings after that. There were only a few blank pages left, and she felt the urge to fill them. There were still so many ways she hadn't captured Teacher. She had him now, but she could never capture what he was to her. That remained in her head, unable to be brought out. She couldn't bring it out of her head, she knew now. She couldn't make him do anything. She couldn't even get him to drink a glass of water or swallow a pill. He was refusing to be what she wanted him to be. He was doing whatever he wanted to do. He was getting so far from himself and from her and she couldn't even stop him. Not even cruelty could stop him.

She had never felt so far from him. She felt closer to him when she was squatting in fields and watching him through binoculars. She felt closer to him when he was in her head. She felt closer to him when she was thinking of him than when she was touching him.

~

The next time she went back to the attic she only looked at him. There was nothing else she could do anymore. She stared hard at him and felt her stomach curl not with affection but with something else. She didn't know what it was she was feeling, but she knew it wasn't a good feeling.

He was still twitching, those strange little bursts of electricity contorting his face and body. He drooled a lot and made noises now too. He mumbled to himself.

She might as well have been looking at a stranger. He certainly wasn't her teacher. He was just a slab of meat. A piece of dead fish still twitching.

Her stomach continued to twist. It felt painful. It felt empty. She could feel it contorting inside her, twitching like he was twitching. It was contorting so much she was beginning to hear it. It was grumbling. Almost like she was hungry.

Her brow creased in confusion. She brought her hands to her stomach.

It was hurting with want of food. With want to fill the emptiness.

She looked at his burns again. They were discolored and weeping now. But beneath the fluids and colors she could see the strange texture of the burns. Just like shredded meat.

The grill had burned him. But had it cooked him?

She knelt before him. With her hand she wiped away the fluids and the medicine cream from his leg. Her touch made him groan and convulse. Like fish parts spasming away from her knife. It was almost like he was feeling her hand on him, but she knew it was only nerves making him dance. She knew he didn't feel a thing.

Carefully, with pinched fingers, she peeled a piece off his leg. He watched her do it, and he groaned as the piece was peeled from him.

She looked at it between her fingers. It was a long, skinny piece, and it was a grayish color, the same gray of cooked meat.

She felt a pressure on her then. She looked up flinchingly and saw him looking at her looking at the meat. It was almost like he was seeing her.

She didn't know if he could see with those eyes. And if he could see, she didn't know if he could process what he was seeing.

His eyes were little mirrors and she saw herself in them. Her reflection was small and distorted.

She shuddered. She turned around. Even if he couldn't see her, she didn't want to see herself. She couldn't stand seeing herself.

She was twitching now, too, not with broken nerves but with a sense of embarrassment. She was embarrassed at herself and what she meant to do.

Her hand moved slowly, uneasily. She put the skinny piece of meat in her mouth.

She wedged just the tip of it between her teeth and took only a small bite. Already, she could taste it. It was exploding with flavor, different kinds of flavor all packed into one. She tasted the bitterness of the medicine cream and the salt of his skin. But more than anything, he was sweet.

She hadn't expected it to be sweet. When one doesn't expect something the mind automatically registers it as unnatural, perhaps gross. Her throat began closing, rejecting it already. The sweetness was almost like the sweetness of decay and rot. But she knew better than to spit it out. She forced herself to keep chewing, tasting.

She put the rest of the meat in her mouth. The meat itself was warm, having just come off his living body, and it was chewy, having not been cooked thoroughly from the grill. It took a while for her to swallow. Her teeth struggled to break it down. And then, as she chewed, the sweetness began to evolve. It was no longer the sweetness of rot, but the sweetness of sugar, candy, dessert.

Was he actually changing or was it her mind making him change again?

Could he be anything she wanted him to be?

She turned around and looked at him. He was looking at her like he knew what she had done even with his damaged brain, even with her back toward him. His eyes were wide and round and set on hers. He almost looked frightened. He almost looked like he had heard her chewing, had noticed the meat was gone. And where else could it have gone other than in her mouth?

He didn't blink. He didn't move. He didn't even twitch. He only looked, and he was looking at her as though she had done something so horrible he couldn't even respond to it. It was like he was going into shock. She didn't think his damaged brain was even capable of going into shock anymore.

Her stomach turned. It didn't feel like hunger anymore. It felt like anger. Frustration.

"What?" she spat at him.

But he still didn't look away. Her throat hurt with frustration about to burst. She was starting to despise him, she realized. He, of all people, she was starting to despise! She didn't know how this could have happened. All she knew was the only thing she liked about him now was how he tasted.

Her face twisted with tears. She felt like she wanted to strike him.

"You're making me not like you anymore," she said.

He said something then. She didn't think him capable of speaking ever again.

"Good," it sounded like he said.

And she did strike him then.

She hit him hard in the face but he only sighed as she did so. It was almost like a sigh of relief.

She sniffed hard as though to get rid of her tears by inhaling them. She wished she liked him the way she used to like him.

Her hand jutted forward to rip off another piece of his leg, for if that was all there was to him, that was what she would take. But as her fingernails dug into his leg, Teacher opened his mouth and screamed something at her.

"Enough!" it sounded like, and he had screamed it louder than he'd ever screamed at her before.

It didn't sound like a word. Perhaps it wasn't a word, just a noise, but she somehow knew what he meant.

She screamed back at him, "That's not nearly enough!"

And he spat at her.

It landed right in her infected eye. One might have thought he had spat acid on her with the way she screamed.

She flailed and shrieked like a madwoman. She was not a girl who shrieked. Her eye burned and she tried to scoop the spit from it, but it clung to her eye. It would never be rubbed out.

She flew at him then. She grabbed a fistful of his leg and the meat just melted and collapsed under her fingers until she could see bone. He screamed like she had screamed. He flailed like she had flailed. He was still fighting against her. He was like a corpse reanimated and more violent than he'd ever been. He knocked his head against hers. His torn forehead touched her own and it felt like a big, wet kiss. The slippery wound was like lips, the hard bone was like teeth. The impact almost sent her flying, and before she could brace herself, he was flinging his knees up as high as he could, kneeing her like they were playing chicken fight. She retreated from his range of violence. She scrambled away to a place where not even his spit could touch her. And now that he couldn't touch her, he began tugging violently at his own wrists. He wrung them, twisted them, yanked at them, and he was making ugly noises all the while, screaming like an animal. Screaming like she had screamed.

The sound of slicing was so loud, it was all she could hear. Like her bird chewing off its own foot.

"Stop!" she screamed, but he wouldn't stop. She no longer heard the slicing of skin, but the grinding of bone. The only thing keeping his hand attached to his wrist was bone.

She grabbed a plastic bag off the floor and went behind him. She put the bag over his head and pulled hard, but he thrashed even harder than the first time. He wasn't her teacher, he was some wild animal.

The bag stretched so far over his face that it broke. It tore a large hole right over his nose and mouth. He gasped for breath now and shook her even harder. Through the hole in the bag, she covered his nose and mouth with her hands, thinking to suffocate him into unconsciousness that way, but he opened his mouth and her hand slipped inside him. Before she could retract it, he was biting her hard.

She shrieked again and sounded more like him than herself. She tried to pull her hand out but he was biting down so hard. It felt like her bones would break, like her fingers would come right off. She felt her skin break already. She felt something hot and wet and couldn't tell if it was her blood or his. With her free hand she struck him in the face, in the head, in the neck, but he wouldn't let go. She bent her free arm and elbowed the top of his head, but he still wouldn't let go. He meant to take her fingers off. He *was* taking her fingers off.

She grabbed his hair and pulled upward with as much force as she could muster. It made his forehead wound tear even further. It was scalping him again and when he screamed she freed her hand. She fell backward onto the floor and writhed there with pain. She looked at her own hand. She couldn't see clearly with only the TV for light and with her soiled, infected eye. She could only see ripped flesh, some white bone, some crooked fingers. It didn't look like a hand. It looked like a slab of meat.

She felt her anger and frustration finally burst inside her. It felt like a part of her was tearing open.

She attacked him again from behind. She wrapped her arms around his neck and squeezed with all she had. It looked like she was hugging him. The blood from his wrists above them fell on them like hot, heavy rain. He thrashed like a fish against her, but he was tiring out. He was growing weak and so was she. She kept clinging to him, squeezing the life from him. She felt him slipping away into unconsciousness or death.

But then the room suddenly became bright.

CUTE AGGRESSION

It was like someone had turned on a light switch or opened the blinds on a window. It made her eyes hurt, and she squinted as she looked over Teacher's shoulder.

The TV had changed.

Teacher was on the screen, not as he was now but as he was in the yearbook.

It was his school portrait. The perfect one. The too beautiful one. It filled the whole TV screen. The white background was like a light and it lit up the room bright like a hospital.

Teacher looked like he was glowing on the TV screen. His skin was so bright, so pale. His teeth were even paler. He was smiling with his teeth and he never did that.

He was so beautiful. He was staring right at her.

She was loosening her grip without even realizing it, and Teacher in her arms was regaining his breath. But he wasn't thrashing anymore. He wasn't fighting. He was only shivering and groaning.

His school portrait on the TV began flashing, and as it flashed Teacher in her arms looked like he was climaxing, but he was only seizing. He convulsed as the TV let out violent bursts of light. He was convulsing so violently she was flung from his body. She looked back and forth between the two of them, between the too-beautiful version of him and what was left of him. Such an ugly sight compared to such a beautiful one. They couldn't have been the same person.

She tried to run to the TV, but she was too unsteady to stand. She crawled instead. She crawled as fast as she could. She pushed the power button, but the TV wouldn't turn off no matter how many times she pressed it. She lunged for the cord then. She unplugged the TV, yanking the cord from the wall so violently a spark flew from the socket. And then the room was pitch black.

She couldn't see anything. She couldn't see Teacher anymore. Neither version of him.

She didn't want to look at him anyway.

~

Teacher was turning in her stomach.

She felt like she was going to throw up but would never throw up. Puking was like sneezing. She couldn't do it if she was too aware of it. Teacher would stay in her like his spit had stayed in her eye, clinging to her just to spite her.

She couldn't shit him out fast enough.

She was uneasy, standing on the platform at the fish factory and afflicted by a nausea that would never ease or burst. She was so nauseous she almost couldn't see. Her eye itched so badly, and she couldn't even scratch it. There was too much fish on her hands. The fish was so cold it burned her hands as she tossed them one by one down into the machine. The fish juices seeped into Teacher's bite marks on her hand. It stung like acid. Like the spit in her eye.

She watched the liquid the fish was turned into, and it was like she was looking into her own stomach. It was like anyone could look down at the machine and see her own stomach.

Though she thought she would never vomit, she suddenly vomited all over the place.

She vomited all over the platform. It was liquid, and she knew Teacher had liquified in her stomach just like the liquid fish in the pot below her. Immediately, she vomited again, and then she nearly slipped in her own vomit. She nearly fell right into the machine. But she felt a hand on her elbow, yanking her backward.

"What's wrong with you, girl?" her mother was yelling as she dragged her off the platform.

She looked up from her own vomit and saw many eyes on her. The eyes of her mother and of all the other factory women. They had seen her vomit. They were looking at her insides dripping all over the platform.

It was just like that time in math class with everyone looking at her dripping with urine.

Her mother began scooping the vomit with her foot, away from the edge of the platform so it wouldn't spill on top of the fish mush. "It almost got into the pot!" her mother said, and then she couldn't bear it anymore. She shook her mother off her elbow. She staggered down the stairs, away from the machine.

Her mother chased after her and grabbed her by the elbow again to stop her.

"What's wrong with you?" her mother said.

"I feel sick," was all she could say.

"You smell sick," her mother said. Then she started sniffing the air around her, confused. "Actually, you smell dead. Is that you?"

She felt another surge of nausea. She couldn't speak.

Her mother kept sniffing her. "Why do you smell like that?"

She tried to force an explanation out of her burning throat, but nothing would come out. She felt like Teacher must have felt.

"Have you been spending time up in the attic?" her mother said.

"*No,*" she managed to spit out, but the way she said the word seemed to override its meaning.

Her mother looked at her knowingly. "I'll take a look for myself when we get home," her mother said.

Her eyes grew wide. "No!" she said. She nearly shrieked it.

Her mother looked surprised at such a noise coming from her.

"That's probably why your eye is infected," her mother grumbled. "There's a ghost in it."

"Mommy, no!" she screamed again, and now the factory women were looking at her instead of her vomit. She felt like she was being crushed by their gazes. She felt like she was being squeezed by a machine until all her juices spilled out.

She ran right out of the factory. She almost slipped in her own vomit to do so.

"What are you doing?" she heard her mother scream at her. The shock in her voice was clear. She had never behaved in such a way before. Her mother might have thought she wasn't even her daughter.

She ran and she didn't stop. Her mother might have been following her. She must have been following her. That was precisely what her mother would do. She would follow her right to the apartment. In her head she imagined her mother bounding up those stairs, storming into that smelly bedroom and seeing Teacher hanging there.

She needed to get rid of him. She didn't wait for a *songthaew*. She ran all the way home. As she ran, night was falling, light was fading. It was quickly getting dark. The wind from her speed whipped at her infected eye, making it sting and itch even worse. It felt like sand was in her eye, but she knew it was only Teacher. She wished it was sand.

She scratched at her eye aggressively as she ran. She scratched it so hard, but that didn't alleviate the itchiness, and the scratching made the same noise that Teacher made when he sliced his wrists open on the fishing line. Yet even so, she couldn't stop scratching. The sound was making her sick and then she was making noises on top of it, noises that scraped against her burning throat. She couldn't hear herself though. She only heard the sound of her eye. She scratched harder and harder, and in her head she thought of Teacher's wrist, of her dead bird, until suddenly she felt something burst. She felt warmth on her fingers, warmth on her cheeks. Her eye was bleeding. She couldn't see.

~

She clutched her eye with her hand. She felt blood pooling in her palm. She felt the hot, slippery warmth of flesh. All flesh felt the same when it was torn. She didn't stop at a mirror to check her eye. She didn't want to see what she had done to herself. She didn't know how bad it was, only that she couldn't see out of that eye anymore. She didn't know if it was blood blinding her eye or if she had scratched the whole thing out. She didn't know if she would find it dangling halfway down her cheek if she looked at her reflection. She didn't want to know.

She stumbled into the apartment building, and as soon as she entered the lobby, she heard a sharp sound, so loud it was like white pain in her eardrums, a tooth pain in her ears.

It was the TV upstairs, so loud it was making the entire building vibrate.

How could the TV be on when she had unplugged it just last night?

She bolted to the attic. She felt like she had felt the first time she had climbed those attic stairs. She felt like she was suffocating, drowning under the weight of Teacher all over again, drowning with the fluid leaking out of her eye. It smelled like the fluids Teacher was leaking.

She crawled on her hands and knees like an animal, blood spilling from her eye like a fountain, a faucet, wetting her path and making her slip. She dragged herself all the way to the closed bedroom door. She could see the TV's light, bright white like hospital lights, spilling out from the gap beneath the door.

She clawed at the doorknob, but when she forced the door open, the light and noise disappeared at once.

The TV wasn't on. It was dark and silent in the room.

The sudden silence was like a noise itself. She squinted through the darkness. She could barely see Teacher hanging there. He looked like nothing but a shape. He was unmoving, slumped like he was sleeping, but his stomach wasn't quivering with breath. His face and body weren't twitching anymore. He looked stiff, unbendable, like a corpse, like he was cold and frozen. He was covered in blood much like the first night. It looked like he was painted in it. It was coming from his wrists. She saw it gushing from him like water from a faucet. He must have been sawing at his wrists constantly.

He might have been dead. He might have killed himself.

She couldn't move him if he was dead. She needed his help if she was going to move him at all. She couldn't move him like she had the first time.

She went to him, crawling on her hands and knees. Up close, he still looked like nothing but a shape. When she reached him she immediately hit his face with a closed hand.

He didn't respond.

She hit him again. Then again. She hit him so hard it was hurting her too. His bones were so hard and sharp against her, she felt her knuckles bruising, but he still would not turn back on. She shoved her fingers down his throat like she had done before. But he still wasn't responding. She didn't feel any breath sucking her hand in. She didn't feel his teeth clamping down on her. She kept desperately digging her hand in him.

And then, the room was suddenly lit.

It was bright white like a hospital, like a yearbook portrait.

But when her head snapped up, she didn't see Teacher's yearbook portrait on the screen. She saw herself.

She lunged at the TV. She hit the power button wildly. It wasn't turning off. She remembered it was unplugged.

It wasn't being powered by electricity. It was being powered by something else entirely.

Her imagination?

She saw herself on the screen. She was in that familiar math class. She was screaming in frustration in front of her whole class, in front of her math teacher. But it wasn't her math teacher. It was Teacher. The too beautiful version of Teacher stood at the front of the class before the math equations on the chalkboard. He stared at her as she screamed. And in the attic she began screaming too. She screamed and clawed at her own face. She smelled urine. She saw it streaming down her legs on the TV screen. She felt it streaming down her legs in the attic. She couldn't tell herself apart from the girl in the TV. She didn't know which one was really her, which world she was really in. Nothing had dimension when seen with only one eye. Everything was as flat as a paper drawing.

Teacher behind her was alive again. He was seizing and groaning again. He convulsed with every flash of light from the TV, and the TV flashed rapidly, on and off, on and off, so fast she couldn't see anything at all. And all the while the TV was screaming her math class scream, deafening and distorted and piercing. It sounded like it came through the terrible intercom at school. It sounded like factory machines, like railway tracks.

She kicked at the screen, but it wouldn't break. She couldn't make it stop. So she scrambled for the hunting knife still on the ground, the one that had taken off Teacher's finger and half his tongue. She flew at him with the knife. She began trying to cut him down, but the fishing line was so deep in his wrists it was like it wasn't even there at all. It was like his wrist had eaten it up.

She had to peel back the skin in order to get to the line. She had to dig her fingers inside him. He was so slippery and warm, all soft, squishy parts like meat, she felt her stomach turning again and it was like he was in her stomach all over again, like she had never vomited him out.

She had the knife deep into his left wrist now, trying to reach the line, when suddenly, amid all the light and the noise, there was a great release.

His left arm fell from the fishing line.

She thought perhaps she had severed the fishing line and released his arm. But when his arm fell, his hand did not come with it.

She had not cut the fishing line at all.

His hand just came off.

She looked at him, at his handless arm now resting between his legs. He was looking at it, too, at the bone jutting from his torn skin.

There was no coming back from this.

"No!" she screeched. It sounded just like the TV sounded. The exact same frustration, despair, humiliation. He was nothing like she thought he would be. He was a children's toy that wouldn't work, a pet fish that kept on dying. There was nothing but meat sitting in front of her, falling apart in front of her. She would dispose of him like meat, then. Let him be flushed down the drain like rotten meat, she thought. Let him be slaughtered like an animal, processed like its meat. He was already dead to her anyway. The teacher in her head was long dead. He was nothing to her. He was nothing to her. He was nothing.

With the hunting knife she cut the fishing line wrapped around his legs. Then she cut the line still holding his right arm. She didn't attempt to cut it at the wrist like she had with his left arm. She cut it about a foot from his wrist, so there would be a good amount of line for her to hold like a leash.

When she severed it, his arm dropped to his lap, joining his disfigured left one. His whole body nearly dropped right to the floor too. Without the line, there was nothing holding him up. She steadied him with her arms, but he was crushing her under his weight all over again.

He didn't seem to know how to unbend his legs. She had to unbend them herself. Then she struggled to help him to his feet. She feared he was too dead to stand. She feared she would have to drag him just like the first night. She yanked hard at the line still attached to his wrist. She pulled him violently, desperately, and then, like some undead thing, he began to rise.

She had forgotten how tall he was. As he stood, it was like he was growing. Suddenly, he was towering over her.

She tugged at the line and began dragging him out of the room. She couldn't wait to be away from this place and its TV still screeching and flashing. Teacher merely followed, moving like a child just learning how to walk. He couldn't seem to stand up straight, or perhaps he had forgotten how to. He remained hunched over, his legs still bent largely at the knees. And as they made their way out of the bedroom and out of the attic, the TV's noise did not fade. It was like it was following them. It was drilling into her ears. She felt her eardrums explode with pain like a toothache. She removed her hand from her eye and covered one of her ears instead.

She pulled him out the door, leading him by the fishing line. They made it down the stairs.

She saw her mother, out of breath, coming into the lobby.

Her face made her look like someone else.

She could see through her mother's eyes. She could see herself standing there on the stairs and bleeding from the eye. She could see herself holding the fishing line attached to Teacher's wrist and leading him like a dog. She could see Teacher beside her, naked and scarcely human, made of swollen parts, missing parts.

"No!" she cried. "Mommy, no!" And her mother remained frozen, clinging to the piss-stained wall with one hand, covering her mouth with the other. She began to sob at what her mother had seen of her. There was no way to explain what her mother saw. She had always been bad at explaining. And she couldn't bear her mother's gaze on her. Sobbing, she gripped the line harder and ran toward the door, dragging Teacher along with her. She ran right through the front door, right past her mother, and her mother did not follow her this time. She only stood there against the lobby wall, looking at her with wide, unblinking eyes.

As she ran into the night and stumbled down the street with

Teacher, she heard her mother's voice behind her, barely a whisper, saying, "What is that?"

~

She dragged him through the streets like a dog. She couldn't tell her noises apart from his. They sounded the same. She saw plumes in the night sky and ran toward them like a beacon. Like a means to an end.

She took him to the fish factory. She couldn't understand how he was still walking, half-dead as he was. But he kept up with her frantic pace, following in her path like her shadow, hunched over with his knees bent like they were still bound. He wasn't her teacher. He wasn't her teacher.

The factory was empty, closed for the night. It was very dark inside the factory. She didn't know where the light switches were. Usually the factory was harshly lit with cold industrial lighting, but now she couldn't see a thing.

The machines were off, but she could still hear the echoing remnants of the TV screaming in her head, loud as the machines themselves. The silence of the factory bothered her. She knew where she was—she had worked here for a year now—but she felt like she was in a different place entirely. Places like this weren't meant to be quiet. She heard Teacher's blood dripping steadily onto the ground. She heard his weird breathing, his weird mumbling.

In the dark she climbed the stairs with Teacher to the second floor where the gutting station was. And then she went to where the shiny new machine was.

She found the light switch. She turned it on.

The shiny new machine was just as ugly as before.

The platform felt unstable as they clambered onto it. It was still slippery with traces of her vomit. She powered the new machine on and it whirled to life. It was impossibly loud, somehow louder when the factory was as silent as it was. She'd never heard anything so loud. It was so loud she couldn't see.

She opened the gate. She guided Teacher over to the edge. He was still looking down at the place where his hand used to be.

"Alright," she screamed to Teacher over the noise. "Get in."

She didn't know if Teacher could hear her. She couldn't even hear herself. Teacher was where she had left him, swaying where he stood, still looking down at his handless wrist.

"Go on," she said. She could hear the despair in her own voice over the noise. "You have to get in."

CUTE AGGRESSION

He looked up from his handless wrist. He looked right at her.

"Don't you want to end it?" she said. "You don't want to go back to your life, do you? Not like this. You don't want people to see you like this."

He kept looking at her. His eyes were blank like fish eyes. He was leaking from so many places. He was dripping all over the platform, just like she had.

She clawed at him then. She tried to push him into the machine to erase him, to eradicate her own thoughts. He was all the thoughts in her head. He was her thoughts put into a human body, one that not only she can see, but everyone in the world can see, even her mother, and she desperately wanted to get rid of him, to hide him from everyone. To look at him was to look straight into her mind, all her secrets, all her desires, all her embarrassments. To look at him was to know everything about her. She was hugging him now. She was crying. She was sucking on his skin. She was wrestling with his body, dragging him toward the mouth of the machine, but he stayed planted, so firm, so strong. Even with parts missing, with parts spilling out, he was heavier than she could manage. He was leaking. His whole body was so wet. He was making a puddle on the platform. It was like her vomit on the platform, and suddenly she felt herself slipping. She tried to tighten her embrace on him, but he was so covered in fluids it was like he was pushing her away. She kept slipping. She was slipping away from him, out of his arms. She was flailing. She was falling right into the machine.

She thought she saw him reach out a hand to her. He had always been kind. But there was no hand attached to his wrist. Only broken flesh and jutting bone. There was nothing to grab on to.

~

A few cans of fish were recalled.

Bits of black hair were found mixed in with the fine fish paste. Something's not right, consumers said. What kind of fish has black hair?

Little threads were found as well, as though from clothing. What kind of fish wears clothes?

The company recalled the batch with apologies.

An investigation would ensue, the company promised.

140

Acknowledgments

To everyone at Grindhouse Press, you've made my dreams come true. I can't thank you all enough for giving this story a chance and for creating a space for boundaries to be pushed.

To my mother, father, and sister, thank you for always loving and supporting me even at my weirdest.

To my parasitic twin, thank you for your endless encouragement. This book wouldn't be what it is without you. You read this book at its most unreadable stages. You saw things in it that I didn't even see. You have helped me more than you know. And I apologize for not adding that one particular scene . . .

And lastly to the readers, I am forever grateful for your time and interest. Sincerely, thank you so much.

Emily Lynn is a Thai-American from California. She works as an English teacher in Thailand. *Cute Aggression* is her first novel.

Other Grindhouse Press Titles

#666__*Satanic Summer* by Andersen Prunty

#100__*Headless* by Scott Cole

#099__*The Killing Kind* by Bryan Smith

#098__*An Affinity for Formaldehyde* by Chloe Spencer

#097__*Kill the Hunter* by Bryan Smith

#096__*The Gauntlet* by Bryan Smith

#095__*Bad Movie Night* by Patrick Lacey

#094__*Hysteria: Lolly & Lady Vanity* by Ali Seay

#093__*The Prettiest Girl in the Grave* by Kristopher Triana

#092__*Dead End House* by Bryan Smith

#091__*Graffiti Tombs* by Matt Serafini

#090__*The Hands of Onan* by Chris DiLeo

#089__*Burning Down the Night* by Bryan Smith

#088__*Kill Hill Carnage* by Tim Meyer

#087__*Meat Photo* by Andersen Prunty and C.V. Hunt

#086__*Dreaditation* by Andersen Prunty

#085__*The Unseen II* by Bryan Smith

#084__*Waif* by Samantha Kolesnik

#083__*Racing with the Devil* by Bryan Smith

#082__*Bodies Wrapped in Plastic and Other Items of Interest* by Andersen Prunty

#081__*The Next Time You See Me I'll Probably Be Dead* by C.V. Hunt

#080__*The Unseen* by Bryan Smith

#079__*The Late Night Horror Show* by Bryan Smith

#078__*Birth of a Monster* by A.S. Coomer

#077__*Invitation to Death* by Bryan Smith

#076__*Paradise Club* by Tim Meyer

#075__*Mage of the Hellmouth* by John Wayne Comunale

#074__*The Rotting Within* by Matt Kurtz

#073__*Go Down Hard* by Ali Seay

#072__*Girl of Prey* by Pete Risley

#071__*Gone to See the River Man* by Kristopher Triana

#070__*Horrorama* edited by C.V. Hunt

#069__*Depraved 4* by Bryan Smith

#068__*Worst Laid Plans: An Anthology of Vacation Horror* edited by Samantha Kolesnik

#067__*Deathtripping: Collected Horror Stories* by Andersen Prunty

#066__*Depraved* by Bryan Smith

#065__*Crazytimes* by Scott Cole
#064__*Blood Relations* by Kristopher Triana
#063__*The Perfectly Fine House* by Stephen Kozeniewski and
        Wile E. Young
#062__*Savage Mountain* by John Quick
#061__*Cocksucker* by Lucas Milliron
#060__*Luciferin* by J. Peter W.
#059__*The Fucking Zombie Apocalypse* by Bryan Smith
#058__*True Crime* by Samantha Kolesnik
#057__*The Cycle* by John Wayne Comunale
#056__*A Voice So Soft* by Patrick Lacey
#055__*Merciless* by Bryan Smith
#054__*The Long Shadows of October* by Kristopher Triana
#053__*House of Blood* by Bryan Smith
#052__*The Freakshow* by Bryan Smith
#051__*Dirty Rotten Hippies and Other Stories* by Bryan Smith
#050__*Rites of Extinction* by Matt Serafini
#049__*Saint Sadist* by Lucas Mangum
#048__*Neon Dies at Dawn* by Andersen Prunty
#047__*Halloween Fiend* by C.V. Hunt
#046__*Limbs: A Love Story* by Tim Meyer
#045__*As Seen On T.V.* by John Wayne Comunale
#044__*Where Stars Won't Shine* by Patrick Lacey
#043__*Kinfolk* by Matt Kurtz
#042__*Kill For Satan!* by Bryan Smith
#041__*Dead Stripper Storage* by Bryan Smith
#040__*Triple Axe* by Scott Cole
#039__*Scummer* by John Wayne Comunale
#038__*Cockblock* by C.V. Hunt
#037__*Irrationalia* by Andersen Prunty
#036__*Full Brutal* by Kristopher Triana
#035__*Office Mutant* by Pete Risley
#034__*Death Pacts and Left-Hand Paths* by John Wayne
        Comunale
#033__*Home Is Where the Horror Is* by C.V. Hunt
#032__*This Town Needs A Monster* by Andersen Prunty
#031__*The Fetishists* by A.S. Coomer
#030__*Ritualistic Human Sacrifice* by C.V. Hunt
#029__*The Atrocity Vendor* by Nick Cato
#028__*Burn Down the House and Everyone In It* by Zachary T.

Owen

#027__*Misery and Death and Everything Depressing* by C.V. Hunt

#026__*Naked Friends* by Justin Grimbol

#025__*Ghost Chant* by Gina Ranalli

#024__*Hearers of the Constant Hum* by William Pauley III

#023__*Hell's Waiting Room* by C.V. Hunt

#022__*Creep House: Horror Stories* by Andersen Prunty

#021__*Other People's Shit* by C.V. Hunt

#020__*The Party Lords* by Justin Grimbol

#019__*Sociopaths In Love* by Andersen Prunty

#018__*The Last Porno Theater* by Nick Cato

#017__*Zombieville* by C.V. Hunt

#016__*Samurai Vs. Robo-Dick* by Steve Lowe

#015__*The Warm Glow of Happy Homes* by Andersen Prunty

#014__*How To Kill Yourself* by C.V. Hunt

#013__*Bury the Children in the Yard: Horror Stories* by Andersen Prunty

#012__*Return to Devil Town (Vampires in Devil Town Book Three)* by Wayne Hixon

#011__*Pray You Die Alone: Horror Stories* by Andersen Prunty

#010__*King of the Perverts* by Steve Lowe

#009__*Sunruined: Horror Stories* by Andersen Prunty

#008__*Bright Black Moon (Vampires in Devil Town Book Two)* by Wayne Hixon

#007__*Hi I'm a Social Disease: Horror Stories* by Andersen Prunty

#006__*A Life On Fire* by Chris Bowsman

#005__*The Sorrow King* by Andersen Prunty

#004__*The Brothers Crunk* by William Pauley III

#003__*The Horribles* by Nathaniel Lambert

#002__*Vampires in Devil Town* by Wayne Hixon

#001__*House of Fallen Trees* by Gina Ranalli

#000__*Morning is Dead* by Andersen Prunty